THE BEST OF
NOT ONE OF US

THE BEST OF

NOT ONE OF US

EDITED BY JOHN BENSON

PRIME BOOKS

CONTENTS

REISEPASS

THE BEST OF NOT ONE OF US

> "How can you be in if there is no outside?"
> —Peter Gabriel, "Not One of Us"

"*Not One of Us* is a collection of stories, poetry, and artwork about people out of place in their surroundings." With those words in the Reisepass (German for "passport") of our debut issue, *Not One of Us* started a twenty-year run, during which we have published two-hundred-and-fifty stories and a like number of poems in thirty-five issues. Here, we have gathered fifteen stories that we think represent some of the very best fiction that appeared in our pages during the past two decades.

We begin with the forbidden child of angel and human in a post-diluvian, post-industrial world, and end with a murderess who mourns her victim's death as it didn't really happen. In between we have a psycho-killer and his brown-eyed girl (David Byrne meets Van Morrison), an understanding woman in the spring of stupidity, dancers drowning and two boys gone too far ("The ghosts of dead teenagers sing to me while I am dancing"—My Favorite).

We meet an outcast who finds her long-sought ideal too perfect, anorexic ghosts of a man's desire ("My whole existence is flawed"—Nine Inch Nails), and a murdered little girl with her f—-ing doll. We go to a coffeehouse where relationships are far stranger than they seem, and a hotel where a woman finds fulfillment aiding aliens. On the home front, we attend matters of family, pre-Terri Schiavo, "tangled up in blue" (Bob Dylan), and witness a rite of passage that works both ways.

Since the magazine's debut in 1986, the purpose of *Not One of Us* has been to consider "otherness" from every possible fictional angle: horror, sf, fantasy, slipstream, mainstream, whatever. Our editorial philosophy reflects my own personal taste in genre fiction. To me the scariest and most deeply moving horror stories are not about monsters or good vs. evil, but rather about the reader's own fears and discomforts. Similarly, for *Not One of Us*, fantasy is not about pseudo-medieval worlds, science fiction is not about space opera. In our zine, it's all about the characters.

We crave characters who are different and act the way they do out of plausible (if occasionally insane) motives. I don't have to like the person: heaven knows we've had some pretty nasty protagonists. But I want to get some insight into her/his/its mind, and vicariously into my own. Also, I like stories, and characters, with *edge*.

"Other" is a nearly universal concept. All groups use "other" to define themselves through exclusion of those who are not like them, so genre, social milieu, and culture do not limit the literary expression of the concept. Exclusion is a painful process most of us have experienced at some time, so that's the starting point for people to understand even more extreme forms of "otherness." And much of the time, "Heaven ain't close in a place like this" (The Killers).

Music has also been an integral part of *Not One of Us*. The Red Hot Chili Peppers captured my mood: "I like pleasure spiked with pain / And music is my aeroplane."

For those (most of you) who have not been following *Not One of Us* from the beginning, I should explain something of its provenance, naming along the way some of the people who have made it possible. I became a fiction editor by accident, but *Not One of Us* was a deliberate act. When I first met (my now wife and associate editor) Anke Kriske, I was a graduate student and she was an aspiring author. In 1984 a story of hers was accepted by Ronny Kaye at a new horror zine called *Doppelgänger*. Soon after that, Anke and I started writing a non-fiction column called "Morbid History and Practice" for the magazine. (She and I are both historians by training, and we used to restore graveyards as a hobby.) Ronny then started sending me manuscripts to read, and when he joined the Peace Corps and left for Niger, he turned the editorship of *Doppelgänger* over to me.

I jumped at the opportunity, but soon I was getting good stories that I couldn't fit into *Doppelgänger* and I began to dream about a publication that was totally our own. I didn't want to do another strictly horror zine; I wanted to get at a theme, the notion of "otherness."

So in early 1986 I let some fellow editors know that I intended to publish a collection that might turn into a magazine. I already had a story ("Chiaroscuro") from William Relling, Jr., that I thought would make a good lead. Then Peggy Nadramia, the editor of *Grue*, sent Wayne Allen Sallee my way with the sequel to a story of his that she was publishing. That sequel, "Take the 'A' Train," joined Relling's story and eleven others in our debut issue, which came out in October 1986. Karl Edward Wagner selected "Take the 'A' Train" for republication in *The Year's Best Horror,* and *Not One of Us* had its first bit of critical acclaim.

In early 1988 I turned over the editorial reins of *Doppelgänger* to Jamie Meyers and concentrated my attention on editing and publishing *Not One of Us.* We soon got a boost in submissions when Ellen Datlow honorably mentioned two stories and a poem from our 1988 issues in *The Year's Best Fantasy* (before "Horror" was added to the collection's title). The next year, Gary Braunbeck's "Matters of Family" (*Not One of Us 5*) was reprinted in *The Year's Best Fantasy and Horror.*

Altogether more than eighty stories and poems from our pages have been reprinted or honorably mentioned in best-of collections (thanks here to Wagner, Datlow, Terri Windling, Kelly Link, and Gavin Grant) or nominated for various awards. As I am not the world's best salesperson, *Not One of Us* has survived for twenty years mainly on its reputation for quality content.

When Sonya Taaffe and I decided to start a *Not One of Us* website two years ago to promote the hardcopy zine, we went back and read all of the issues from 1986 to the present. (We were not yet thinking about a *Best of Not One of Us*.) We were both surprised at the underlying consistency of theme, even as the magazine evolved.

I consider *Not One of Us* to be an expression of my soul, and I don't often allow people into its workings. There have been three important exceptions. Anke, of course, has been there since the creation, not only of *Not One of Us*, but also of our sons, Karl and Derek. She continues to second-read and put up with the quotidian hassles of dealing with a magazine and with me.

Tina Reigel breathed new life into *Not One of Us* as associate editor from 1992 to 1996. In particular, she tightened the theme and added freshness to the musical backdrop. Tina was the only person associated with the magazine who also played an important role in my professional life, teaming with me on surveys about end-of-life issues.

Finally, without Sonya Taaffe this book would not have been possible. Sonya has also made me much more aware of the opportunities afforded by fantasy to address the concept of "otherness."

I would also like to thank my son Karl Benson for acting as technical advisor on the magazine the past two years. In addition he designed and serves as webmaster of our website (http://not-one-of-us.com).

I would be remiss if I did not thank two important groups of people who are not represented here: the poets and artists who have played a crucial part in our magazine's success. Also, acknowledging that we were unable to include more than a small proportion of the best *Not One of Us* stories in this collection, I want to thank all those whose prose fiction has graced our pages. Sometimes during the selection process I felt like Buridan's Ass, equidistant from two carrots, yet at risk of starving to death from being unable to make a rational choice about which one to eat.

I hope you enjoy the feast that follows.

John Benson
Natick, Massachusetts

ANOTHER COMING

SONYA TAAFFE

death's angel is my cousin but I never said
he was my favourite relative
      —Phyllis Gotlieb, "Doctor Umlaut's Earthly Kingdom"

Rain was still falling when she stepped off the tracks, walking the old railroad under a sky like newsprint too sodden to read. Down a bank of gravel and clinker, small scraping crunches underfoot as Acacia stepped carefully in the slick weather, the cool slanting mist that clung in her hair and made her skin feel clammy, spongy as something drowned; she could not wipe it off. The air smelled of earth, dark and chill, and faintly of smoke and iron. Freight echoes, from a time when these rails and ties had rattled daily under flatbeds, sleepers, ores and travelers stitching cities together; but the stitches had come out and only steel scars remained behind for Acacia to walk the right of way, a small tight-shouldered figure against the stingy trees, malt-colored hair trailing out of its braid and her eyes a little warmer than the wet bark around her in the cloud-melted light. Her stomach hurt, turned over and in on itself; she put both hands in the pockets of her long coat, Leo's borrowed oilskin, away from the insistent feeling of something minute and irretrievable—a fleck, a grain, pearl-grit—lodged deep within her flesh. *A riddle in nine syllables.* She would need several more to explain this.

Here the trains' cargo had come, where the trees gave onto a yard of scabbed asphalt and the buildings that had stood cold for longer than Acacia had been alive. Some abandoned industry, the shell and skeleton of a steel-driving age: high brick walls and each grid of close-set windows cracked inward or outward, cloudy glass still clinging in the frames like old ice, panes of glaucoma; skylights fallen in around the steel braces, flat stretches of tarry gravel for the remaining roofs and some of the gutters still copper and sallow green. Even the company's name, high on one time-blackened face of brick, had worn off over the neglected decades; ground to illegible traces of block-lettered paint, replaced by graffiti, ivy, and the amorphous scripts of lichen and acid rain. Acacia had never seen anyone else inside, though sometimes she found the leftovers of trash-barrel fires below the catwalks and flaking presses, the detritus of bottles and cans as everpresent as dust or oxidation. Only Quince, or Leo, or herself: footsteps in oil stains and shadow, disturbing a country of obsolescence and rusted memory.

Quince was smoking under the scant overhang of a loose gutter, birch-bleached hair shaved down to pinfeather fuzz and her eyes half-closed against the shapeless, watercolor light. Black raincoat wrapped to her knees, heeled boots strapped and buckled mid-calf, she made an incongruous package among the corroded, autumn-colored wreckage: one foot angled up against the rain-worn bricks, the other planted in weeds and ash-brown grasses; rain dripped past her shoulders and she turned her head slightly at Acacia's approach, no more movement anywhere than that, no more sound than the wind dividing itself through broken teeth of glass, empty doorways and the spaces where stairs used to be.

"I thought you might have come out here first." She dropped her other foot to the ground and came forward just enough to meet Acacia: a needless, neighborly gesture. All the bones of her face were exact, fluid, fared into one another as adroitly as joinery or etching, expressions done silverpoint on her pale skin. She moved in a cloud of cloves and old burning, like incense in the matte folds of her coat and her fine, close down of hair where rain glittered now; under the smoke, her skin gave off its own edged musk that made Acacia think, not unpleasantly, of civet cats and other predatory, perfumed creatures. "Every now and then, I'm wrong. But you've made me right, now that you're here yourself—what have you done with Leo?"

"I was going to ask you that." Even as she tried to make the words into a smile, Acacia heard them pouncing, defensive, the question spun too quickly back at Quince in her private atmosphere of silver-streaked air and smoke. Her pulse was jammed in her throat, a dam for words. She considered asking Quince for a drag, an old nervous reflex that still dried the back of her mouth; but Quince was stubbing out her cigarette against the brick, and Acacia had never smoked after high school. "He left late last night, before you got back. Before I thought you'd get back," wondering briefly where Quince had slept, in whose arms, and how it never mattered. Leo and Acacia, the two faces of Quince's coin: one was as true as the other. Tears burned abruptly behind her eyes and she said, "I haven't seen him all morning. We had a conversation. I thought you might have."

"No." Restless, Quince knocked one heel against the cindery ground, looked slantwise at Acacia. In the overcast, drowned-grey clarity of light, she had a child's lucid complexion; blackish brows and lashes limning her eyes like a mask. "But tell me how you're using that word *conversation*. It has uneasy echoes."

The words were easier to say than she had feared: repetition, she thought bitterly, practice. "I'm pregnant." Dead air; rain on industrial ruins. "We talked about that."

At a distance, Quince's eyes were indefinitely dark; up close, they changed and became differentiable, shades and textures of dark, as telling and legible as a blush, a pallor, a frown. Her voice was as impenetrable as the bricks at her back. "It must be his."

Leo's skin, like honey in the light, silk and ivory in the dark; all the words of sculpture and artistry that she used even as shorthand for sensation, the touches and tastes of him, long watered-honey eyes and the feel of hard velvet under her hand; and Quince, laughing above or below them, her small breasts and her scars and her graceful hips, entering, entered, her seed as sharply aromatic as her flesh— Acacia shook her head. "I'm not sure."

"You can't have mine." Now Quince was shaking her head, denial in return; she had a silver stud in her left ear, gold in her right. *My brother, good morning: my sister, good night . . .* Her voice tipped slightly, a note sharp. "It's got to be his."

Acacia discovered her arms crossed low, almost around her belly and the invisible weight within, and jerked them back to her sides. "I said, I'm not sure." Her voice had gone ragged much faster than she expected, the unreliable ease flaking from her words like rust or dried blood, chips of brick from the wall that Quince slammed her hand up against, flat-palmed, percussive smack of meat and she swore between her teeth as Acacia said fiercely, "I haven't had any tests done—"

"You can't!" Only in bed, in the warm chaos of caring and desire, had Acacia seen Quince as unguarded, as intense: perhaps as frightened. "You fucking can't, Acacia. Not my child. It's not—"

"Not what, possible?" Between breath and word, she was shouting. Catching fire from each other, reflecting like always: she no longer felt the cold. "You're not any more possible, what does that matter? Quince, it's either yours or Leo's, and it's mine!" Less than five minutes, and things were already splintering: *the center cannot hold* and the poetry, immediate and familiar as a second language, was no comfort now. Quince shook her reddening hand, stared at Acacia. Rain sharpened on brick and battered glass, the sound of knives. "It doesn't matter," Acacia said quietly, around the hurt in her throat that might have been shouting and might have been her heart, "how much you want it not to be true. You can leave, Leo can leave. But I'm still pregnant. Tell me later why you don't want it. I don't really want to talk anymore right now."

She kicked aside a thin rubble of broken concrete as she walked away, dry clatter and a metallic ricochet off the grating up ahead; the nearest set of doors stood ajar, unlocked slabs that ground orange-rind rust into her palms as she pulled them open, damp and a deserted, erosion smell in the soot-colored shadows beyond. Dishwater light crossed overhead, filtered through broken layers onto metal beams and disused machineries, the good salvage and scrap sold long ago. She did not think she had really expected Quince to follow her. Still she looked back, through the doorway to the space where Quince was no longer smoking, once: neither salt nor dead shade, but the underworld that trapped, the burning disaster.

She had walked home from the clinic in rich, late afternoon, clouds like rough marble shoaled above the skyline for the sun to slide around and turn the air to fire. Pigeons rose up from the roofs, the flock lifting in one noisy-winged, furling curve against the sky; a skinny tree on the corner, potted in cement and spoked iron, was putting out buds that Acacia stopped and fingered for a moment, germination swelling cool and rough under her touch. Even the storm grate smelled like approaching spring, clean and humid, as she passed. *Do you want to make a follow-up now?* the doctor had asked, a neat short-haired woman as bristly grey as a fledging bird, and Acacia had ducked her head and mumbled something indistinct about talking to the father, getting back to her; the sickly knot in her stomach winding tighter and colder as the woman spoke, and she wondered if morning sickness would give her enough excuse to throw up on the white-tiled floor. A promise got out of her mouth instead, *I'll call tomorrow.* Keys cold in her hand, she unlocked the front door and went up without turning on the light, bare bulb hanging in a sphere of silver wires at the top of the stairs, aesthetically caged.

Leo was at his desk in the living room, among the more portable and less fragile aspects of his work: assistant curator buried in manuscripts and orreries and cracked icons, cataloguing, cleaning, running for coffee, and sometimes his glasses had a fur of dust around the rims. He twisted around in his chair at the click of the lock, one arm braced across the over-stuffed back, a manila folder in his other hand raised in familiar, puzzled salute; the long-sleeved T-shirt he wore, *If you're a Goth, where were you when we sacked Rome?* in white capitals on black, Acacia had bought for him when he got the museum job. *There's tea in the kitchen,* he said easily, as if he had not expected her home much later, *but it's herbal;* and when she only stood with her jacket in her arms, staring at the hardwood joins underfoot—polished with years and bare feet, the color of fresh bread, and she thought about kneeling to lay her hand against their fine-grained shine and feel where the cracks were—he put down the folder and walked across the small carpets until he could put his hands on her shoulders and ask, *Acacia? What happened?* No good way to start the conversation, though her skin flamed under his palms; no beautiful seams of language for this moment. Haltingly, she said, *I went to the doctor's,* and watched Leo's expression change.

Light like antique gold sloped through the window and made his hair a corona, his face a painted mask of the sun: a frustrated summer-god, a bewildered star. But constellations never stared down from heaven and said, *Oh, fuck. Weren't we safe? Didn't you use anything? I always—oh, fuck. Fuck. I can't deal with this,* and Acacia had never seen a solar myth come to adolescent pieces before her eyes. She tried to touch him, his name thrown out like a line for him to hold, *Leo,* but he was too lost in some nightmare of responsibility, already running too far and too fast for anything other than distant light to reach him. *I have to think about this,* he said, sometime much later when she had run out of tears, cried herself into a sore throat and spasms that he would have soothed any other time, if she had been crying for any other reason. Instead she curled in a feral tangle of sheets and tried to pin her breath down again, gulping, dry-heaving tears, head buried in her arms to keep him out of her peripheral vision. *Acacia; Acacia? Listen to me, Acacia, please, I have to think about this. I have to talk to Quince. I have to—oh, my God, I have to talk to my parents. I can't. I'm sorry, I'm so sorry,* and she heard the bedroom door shut even before he finished saying *sorry.*

She must have slept; she woke to dull cloud-light, mouth sticky and salt grit in her eyes, the blinds making tambourine noises in a wind that tasted of storms. When she sat up, the emptiness of the apartment settled around her as the chill had not. She got out of bed in a movement as convulsive as a shudder. With oils and a fine brush, Quince had half-blinded all the apartment's mirrors, so that Acacia's passing reflection looked back in slices and fragments from among brilliant, blasphemous tableaux. In a glade of burning green leaves, a naked woman accepted a crimson globe mouth-to-mouth from an androgyne plumed in rainbow-slick scales; another woman stood, bloody-handed, one fist still clenched around an ear of pulped, dripping grain, above her sister sprawled in her sacrifice's blood; sheep, horses, flailing human figures sank beneath choking cobalt waves that tossed afloat a ship full of fabulous, archaic beasts. Over the dresser in the bedroom, a female figure whose wings were made of flames and calligraphy stooped like a hawk to embrace a male figure that looked upward, dumbstruck, lovestruck, ready. *Gaze no more in the bitter glass:* as if her heart would have given her any better suggestion.

She smelled Quince before she heard her lover's boots on the cement, musk and sweet burning almost tangible from where she stood; she unbent from memory slowly. Spray-painted tags littered this side of the wall, the browned scaffolding overhead and the nailed-up plywood blocking another door: an archaeology of graffiti, vivid strata she could not read. Once Leo had pretended to translate some for her, charting the dynastic rise and fall of urban legends. Apple-green glass fanned in a brittle, glinting spray about her feet. Without turning her head, Acacia said, "Why don't you want a child?"

Quince's voice was a breath at her back, glancing, recitative, not soothing. "When men began to increase on earth," she said, "and daughters were born to them, the sons of God saw how beautiful the daughters of men were, and took wives from among those that pleased them . . ." Glass cracked under her heel; half a step away, Acacia felt Quince's nearness working its way into her own skin, loosening muscles, burnishing nerves, until she waited for Quince's mouth at the curve of her neck, telling story into her skin, Quince's hands holding her close against hard-budded breasts and the press of desire at her groin. She had always courted Acacia with myths and mysteries. Still she held herself tightly away from even the air that eddied around Quince, breathing rain and spices and the familiar scents that meant comfort, need, companionship:

nothing safe. Leo had smelled like sweet salt and brittle pages, and that had not stopped him. Then Quince's voice slanted, wryer and less ritual—"The sons of men were also pretty beautiful"—and something untwisted beneath Acacia's breastbone. That first day, summer in the creamy marble shadow of the museum where Leo did not yet work, where Acacia was looking at Leighton and Rosetti, Quince had given her the same sideways truth: the low-voiced speaker coming up behind her as she perused studies for John Singer Sargent's *Annunciation* and Acacia turning around to interrupt, *Unless I've really got the story wrong, it's not Gabriel's kid,* and look at Quince, and consider whether Mary had ever wished otherwise.

Rain dripped through cracked slates and girders, little sounds in the hollow space, as negligible as the details of Quince's strangeness had always been: inexplicable and no one asked for answers. But Acacia had one already, that she had not wanted to hear. She said, a thin ache of a word, "So?"

"So," Quince said, "so," and nothing else.

Glass shone under both their feet, little more than reflection and razor edges in the dimness. Acacia's fingers twisted in her hair, under her braid where loose, rain-curled strands had inked themselves to the back of her neck; one snapped and pain wired into her scalp, and she had to close her throat against the sound that wavered too close to tears for the minor, momentary hurt. Under Quince's regard or indifference, and she would not know unless she looked, she felt scraped raw at the surface, pressures inside and outside wearing her to little more than a shivering handful of tears wrapped around less than a handful of life. *Some kneeling girl with passionless pale face,* that museum afternoon. She wanted desperately not to say whatever would come next; she took her hand out of her hair, and turned around.

Quince's eyes were the darkness of desolation, sounded and known, and water brimmed along her lower lids. The clotted light turned her skin to dusted stone, ancient paper, blank; she looked neither old nor young but unreal, and a sudden chill sank in Acacia's stomach. At once, she wanted the tagged bricks to crumble dryly, let her through as she backed against them and out into the drowning, rain-swept day; she wanted to lean forward and lick at the sweat shining at Quince's temple, salt and the crisp, feathering brush of Quince's hair against her lips; or, simplest of all, to uncross her arms and open them so that Quince, if she wanted, could move into their circle and rest there until she was no longer terrifying, terrified, full of tears. But Quince was saying, "It's not safe," and Acacia would be dead and dust before light crossed that space between them.

"Not safe how?" she asked anyway, because she could not touch Quince and Leo had never waited to have this conversation. "For me? Or you mean the child?" Quince's arms were as tightly folded as Acacia's, pale fists tucked under black-leather elbows; her mouth admitted nothing. "Quince . . . You keep saying *can't*, like that fixes everything. But if there's any chance, if there's some kind of problem, you have to tell me. If I carry this child, if it's yours, is there going to be something wrong with it? It'll have birth defects, it'll be retarded, psychotic," she was biting off the words like bitter stalks, "what?"

"Like me," Quince said tautly, "and like you. And that's forbidden."

"What?"

"They drowned in the Flood, all the children of men and angels. And there have been no more since. All the beautiful monsters"—one corner of her smoky mouth crooked upward, very slightly—"long before Leo's reliquaries and papyri, those ferns and fossils down the block—or maybe long after or somewhere in between. Somewhere else, it doesn't really matter. Here, now: no more. The universe would not permit it. The laws of physics and angels don't allow."

A desert in her mouth: teeth to tongue to palate like a cleavage of dust and wax. "You're grander than Leo, after all. He only thinks this will destroy his life."

"It's raining," Quince whispered. Her face was not an icon. When she moved forward, tines of shadow passed over her face like expressions, writing, rewriting; a palimpsest. "Not by water, not again—there was a promise. But still, it keeps me thinking. Oh, my love," and her hands touched Acacia's shoulders so lightly that she might have been an echo of Leo, a ghost frozen to this conversation in a flash of time. Recursive, while it rained: a shiver went like a shockwave over Acacia's skin and she could not imagine that Quince had not felt it. One hand angled briefly upward to cup the back of Acacia's head, fingers sliding through her tight-gathered hair; returned to her shoulder, the point of her pulse, blood for two circling through her veins now. "Oh, God. Acacia. It had better not be my fucking child."

The air smelled of ozone and myrrh. Quince's thumb caressed the shallow rise of her collarbone, sweet dry warmth against her sweating skin; the movement relaxed Acacia no more than Quince's remote gaze, the change of dark in her eyes that Acacia could not read. Something pushed hard into her throat, horror or laughter; words came out instead. "Stop this. Just stop. You and Leo . . . I haven't been struck by lightning; his parents haven't disowned him; I don't care. Let it be nobody's child. Just mine. There's nothing else to say."

"You don't understand. I love you," and before Acacia could answer, Quince's hands stilled. She might have smiled like this for the sight of world's end, a sky full of fire and ash. "I can't even take the chance."

Acacia drew breath to shout again, and stopped. "Quince—" But Quince's fingers were pressing silence into her throat, tightening with less pain than burning where she should have breathed and a distant, gathering roar like thunder rending the air open, a wave toppling toward the shore. Her vision swam red and dark: the blind landscape of the womb. "Don't . . ." She could not even hear the noises she made.

"If you aren't sure, I can't. Please." Quince's voice heaved like Acacia under her hands, driven and cornered, trapped as the breath that she could not catch; her shoulder struck plywood, glass bit into her knees, and she could as easily have wrenched free of Quince as her heart from her bursting chest. She could not see Quince's face clearly anymore, nor the ruined walls beyond, old before Acacia was born and how many cities had Quince seen rise and fall? Her lungs threshed for air. The fountains of the deep; forty days' deluge. Nothing to salvage, this time. "Just tell me it's Leo's."

Her fingers pried at Quince's wrists, like clawing at marble with her nails. There was nothing in her left to whisper with, no air, no thought; she heard her own voice like something pinched from sand, from the gravel ballast scattered beneath the old tracks that she had followed here, a path of stones into darkness. "It could be Leo's," and before the fingers could loosen, her vision clear and the choking fire in her throat turn to air again, she got the words out. "And it could be yours."

The darkness crushed down on her.

But now I know

That twenty centuries of stony sleep

Were vexed to nightmare by a rocking cradle . . .

Rain was falling on her face, freshwater cold that tasted faintly bitter as tarpaper and smoke, salt drops warm as the amniotic sea where a pearl of flesh drifted, moored between worlds. Far above her, against the wrung-out wash of sky and shrouded sun, someone was saying, "Fuck me," over and over, like a prayer. Her throat was full of cinders. Half in Quince's arms, her head fallen back against Quince's shoulder and a freezing glaze of rainwater seeping into her jeans, Acacia blinked and tried to speak, made a noise like breath ceasing. Quince's arms tightened around her, eased as she struggled, spasmodic in a terror that sluiced out of her as abruptly as her strength; she heard Quince's voice, half-crying and hasty, "I won't, fuck me to God, Acacia, I won't!" and a different darkness slipped up over her before she tasted Quince's tears again.

She opened her eyes to clouds like wet slate, sun sliding toward evening and the rain still as cold, Quince's arms wrapped close about her and her throat just enough less ravaged for Quince's name. It might have been a question.

"I don't know." This voice had never whispered to her in bed, in a museum, over tea; Quince had never shivered like this. Answer and denial at once, "I don't know. If it's mine . . ."

Acacia said softly, "Mine." As suddenly and unconditionally as a small child, she wanted Leo; she wondered if he would hold her through that word, single and irrevocable; if it would make a difference. "The others?"

Quince's throat jerked, a swallow of nothing like a flinch. "I have no children."

A scrape of ash in her mouth. "You *are* a monster."

One of Quince's brows raked an amused, caustic angle; she bent as though to kiss Acacia's forehead, stopped. "I've never been anything else. Not in this world, how could I be?" Her face was very quiet. "And you never thought I was."

"No . . ." Acacia shifted in Quince's arms, enough to see her profile like weather-carved stone against the flat brick facade, punched-out windows and hanging gutters, motionless as rain traced her parted lips: a gargoyle from a painted mirror, a shadow of cataclysm at the back of her eyes. The question faded on her tongue, unasked; she said instead, "I don't accept a God that would ruin the world for anything as beautiful as your child."

Momentarily, Quince's smile was real and rare as a falling star. "As beautiful as your child, too. You've never believed that: that you are beautiful. I must have told you enough times. You and Leo, you amaze me, always. Even now." The smile slid away with the rain. "Especially now." Wind drew damp nails over Acacia's skin and she waited beneath Quince's silence, her gaze as distant as when Acacia had come up to her beneath the gutter, centuries ago, no time at all: the messenger. "This I know: fire, water, fucking locusts, it doesn't matter in the end. This place, that you like so much? Times change. Everything falls apart, sooner or later—rusts, dies, dissolves, decays—and nothing, no matter how cunning, how profitable, how lovely, lasts." Quince's voice was very soft, her body where Acacia leaned very still. "Nothing."

"Yes," Acacia said, as softly. "I know." But she lay in Quince's arms anyway, for this moment, and they watched the rain fall.

THE ELEVATOR

PATRICIA RUSSO

The first time Danton saw the girl on the elevator, he didn't know she was dead. Neither did I. Danton told me about the encounter in that quiet, controlled way he had, barely raising his voice; a thin white line around his lips gave the only hint he was upset.

"Eight years old. Maybe nine. She was wearing these dirty sneakers, I mean really filthy. That was the first thing I noticed, how dirty her sneakers were."

Danton was a compact guy, not much taller than me, in shape but no big gym rat. It was weird to see him fighting to hold himself still, not pacing back and forth because it might stir up the old lady who lived below me. All his muscles were tensed, as if he wanted to hit something, someone. I'd never thought of Danton in connection with physical violence before. Okay, so maybe that thought crosses your mind about every guy. But I'd never associated it with him so closely, seen him as so capable of it, not in the eight months we'd been together.

"She doesn't live in the building. I've never seen her before."

"Could be somebody's grandkid," I offered. I still had no clue where this was going. Sprawled on the couch—unsexy, but it'd been a long day, and Danton had seen me way worse—a textbook oozing with academic bullshit face down on my belly, I was giving him my full attention. I have a bad habit, though, of interrupting people, finishing their sentences, trying to help them get their thoughts out, that kind of thing. Danton was still working stuff through in his mind; as soon as I spoke, I knew I shouldn't have. He twitched his shoulder. I shut up.

"She was filthy, too. She stank, Melanie. When the elevator doors closed, I almost choked. And her hair . . ."

I kept quiet. After a moment, he continued.

"I could feel her staring at me. A kid that little shouldn't be allowed to ride the elevator alone. I didn't want to turn around. I wasn't going to. But she started saying, 'Mister, mister, look,' and I, you know, I glanced over my shoulder. She had a toy, some kind of cheap knockoff Barbie." Danton's voice shook slightly.

Closing the book without bothering to mark my place, I set it on the floor and swung my legs over the side of the couch.

Danton's face was rigid, his fists clenched, but his voice was still soft. "'Look, mister, look, mister,' she said. She ripped the doll's dress up and scissored its legs up and down. Jerking them. Pumping them. You should've seen the expression on this kid's face, Melanie. It was evil. 'Look, mister, dolly-fucking!' and she shoved the damn thing at me."

My mouth opened automatically.

Danton wasn't finished. "I hit the floor buttons. All of them. As soon as we stopped I jumped out. I walked the rest of the way up."

"Wow," I said.

"Eight years old. Eight goddamn years old."

I put my arms around him. His whole body was as taut as a stretched wire.

"Fucking kids."

"Come on," I said, rocking him a little. "It's okay. Let's go to bed."

"I could've strangled her."

I nudged him into the bedroom. Danton stripped off his clothes mechanically and dropped his lean length on my futon without enthusiasm. We were sleeping back to back tonight; I could see that without a crystal ball. The last thing he said to me before sleep took him was, "I could've killed that damn kid."

I still thought, that night, that the child Danton had seen on the elevator was the granddaughter of one of the tenants. The building was old, pre-war, and so were some of the residents. We had a mix of rent-controlled, pension-collecting oldtimers and grad students and ex-grad students paying market rates; an interesting mix, I felt. The wrinklies were friendly. They ran the place, really, organizing parties, picnics in the garden we shared with the building next door, even star-gazing gatherings on the roof, complete with telescopes. Most of them had interesting stories to tell, too. One old guy who lived on the first floor, Mr. Dane, claimed to have once owned a cat who lived to be thirty; during the sixties Mr. Dane and his pals used to drop acid and follow the cat around on their hands and knees, seeking enlightenment. He showed me a photo of the cat in a chased-silver frame. The cat's name was Elliott. One more object lesson on why you shouldn't do drugs, I thought, though of course I didn't tell Mr. Dane that.

So I believed the filthy, foul-mouthed child was just some everyday spoiled precocious brat bored with making nice to grandpa or grandma.

I was wrong.

Two days later, I saw her myself.

I hadn't expected to. Why would I? I'd already almost forgotten Danton's odd little only-in-America vignette. I was hauling grocery bags, two in each hand—Dad had actually come through on one of his oft-promised, seldom-written checks, and I'd lost my head just a tad at the SuperBuy—and my mind was churning in slow futile circles around a problem in transformational generative grammar and at the same time wondering why Danton hadn't called—he lived in the same building, two floors above me, and lots of times he didn't call or even e-mail because, as he said, "We see each other every day," only we didn't, and . . .

I didn't see the little girl when I stepped on the elevator. There was a completely rational explanation for that. I was distracted. I was lost in thought. My mind was elsewhere.

I knew, though, the way you absolutely know something like that, that the elevator had been empty when I got on.

Somewhere between the second floor and the third, I noticed the smell.

The stink, actually. A putrid, gut-curdling reek of crap and corruption, a dung-heap stench. I might have been a city girl, but I'd spent every summer of my interminable childhood in the country, so I know from dung and heaps, up close and personal. I coughed, instinctively, and the cough nearly turned into a retch. Dropping the grocery bags, I raised my hands to cover my nose and mouth.

I heard a small voice behind me. "Look?"

Timid, quavering, questioning. High-pitched, unmistakably a child's voice.

"Look?" Pleading.

Weirdly, stupidly, I didn't think of Danton's story, his experience (the white line around his lips) until I turned. Then I saw the kid, and it all came back to me with the force of a roundhouse blow.

She was filthy, all right. This was a little girl who hadn't had a bath for a year. Maybe years. Her clothes were rotting off her, and those sneakers—those once-white, supermarket-aisle canvas sneakers—shit, they should've been frigging *burned*.

Oh my god, I thought, horror stories from psych class popping into my mind, feral children, kids kept in closets by nutcase parents, strapped to long-outgrown potty chairs, chained to radiators . . .

The little girl looked at me. Her eyes were wary, scared. I wanted to drop to my knees and hug her, tell her it was okay, that everything would be all right. I didn't move.

She was clutching something in her grimy hands, holding on to it with a death grip. A cheap plastic doll in a pink sequined dress so old and ratty most of the sequins had fallen off. So cheap the arms and legs were hollow—almost transparent—and unbendable at the knees or elbows.

I could've said something.

What? "What's your name?" No. "Hi. My name is Melanie. What's yours?"

I couldn't make my mouth move.

The girl crept forward. Under the dirt, her hair was the same color as the doll's, an almost golden blond. The smell that rose from her was hideous.

Tentatively, fearfully—if I knew anything, understood anything, it was that this kid was scared shitless—she drew the doll's dress up to expose its hairless, smooth, unreal crotch. Slowly, the girl moved the doll's legs back and forth. "Look," she whispered. "Dolly-fucking."

The elevator door opened on my floor. I fled. Like a coward, a fucking coward. I retained the presence of mind to grab my groceries, my freaking gourmet-aisle items, before I ran out and pounded down the hall and almost got the key jammed in the lock and slammed the door open and slammed it shut and locked and bolted everything that could be locked or bolted.

My heart was hammering harder than it ever had in my life.

I put the groceries away.

That might be the thing that makes me cringe the most, the thing I most don't want to think about. I snatched up my groceries and I put them away. Everything neat and tidy and in its proper place. Yeah.

Then I started pacing. Not thinking. Not thinking. Very deliberately and determinedly not thinking, and not giving a rat's crap about the old woman below me who liked to bang on her ceiling with a mop handle or *some*thing when she felt I was making too much noise. I paced until the sweat was running down my neck.

I looked out the window of the front room—looked out and looked down—and saw Danton in the garden. He wasn't alone; a bunch of the Elder Ones were sitting in lawn chairs, Mrs. Sayce, Mrs. Blomberg, Mr. Dane. I noticed them, but I didn't truly see them. I saw only Danton, leaning against the ivy-spotted, barbed-wire-topped concrete wall that shielded the little garden from the street, his hands shoved deep into the front pockets of his jeans. His body language separated him from the others: back turned, head tilted down, eyes on the ground.

I ran to him.

I took the stairs.

Racing out into the garden, I grabbed Danton and squeezed him tight. Almost choked the life out of him, I was so weirded out. He hugged me back. I have to give him that.

You have to give him that.

I babbled out the story. Some of it. The girl in the elevator, the doll – Danton's face went stony.

I didn't get half of what I needed to say said. Not even a quarter of it.

He stiffened, pushed me away—not meanly, not angrily—well, not angry at me—but as soon as he heard *doll* he swung around to glare fire at the oldies in their plastic-mesh green-and-white lawn chairs.

"Who is this kid?" he snapped. "You know who we're talking about. She's in the building all the time, she has to belong to somebody."

Mrs. Sayce and Mr. Dane looked entirely blank. Mrs. Blomberg was a poorer actor. Her face colored, and all of a sudden she got real interested in her shoes.

"It's a disgrace," Danton said, his voice rising. Danton never raised his voice. "The girl's a menace. She needs to be in therapy, or locked up or something. You know what I'm talking about." He swept a bitter, accusatory gaze over the oldsters. Mrs. Sayce might have flinched.

The sun was out, but I felt cold. "Danton—"

"That child needs to be controlled."

Mrs. Blomberg had gone quite still. Something in her face deepened the chill in my stomach to ice. "Danton, let's go inside."

"They know," he insisted. "They have to."

"Son," Mr. Dane said slowly, "I'm sorry, but I have no idea what you mean," and Mrs. Sayce took the cue and nodded, her white head bobbing like a jack-in-the-box puppet on a loose spring.

"Come on." He didn't want to, but I tugged on his arm until, with a short, disgusted sigh, he turned and followed me back into the apartment building.

I hesitated before heading for the elevator. Actually we both did, but when it came we got on, the dingy-walled chamber empty except for us, no smell except the usual stale air and a faint hint of someone's dime store aftershave. Danton kept shaking his head, like, can you *believe* this.

In the apartment—mine—I almost brought the subject up a couple of times. I caught myself though, held back, waiting. Danton opened the fridge, shut it again, rummaged through the kitchen cupboard, picked up a package of super-premium from-actual-Scotland shortbread cookies, put them back again.

"Somebody should do something," he said. Quiet-voiced. The white line was around his lips again. "Kids like that have to be kept under control."

"Danton—"

His name hung in the air; I let it stay there until he stopped fiddling with a box of crackers and looked at me.

"Danton, do you think she was alive?"

He put up a good front for a minute, but the edges of the façade crumbled way before he gave up the effort. I took the box of crackers from him and opened it.

"What do you think?"

"I think she wasn't." Two cylinders of stoned-wheat crackers. The waxy paper wrappers wouldn't come off either of them. "Isn't."

"Hey." Lightly. Trying to make light of it. "Since when have you believed in ghosts?"

She hadn't been in the elevator when I got on. The smell of her—or the smell that accompanied her—had appeared twenty or thirty seconds after the doors closed.

"I don't know. What time is it?"

Danton tried to laugh.

It wasn't funny, though, not at all.

We had dinner, sort of, and sex, even more sort of, and then Danton said he was going back up to his place. I'd been wanting to talk more, about the little girl, about . . . about what to *think* about a dead child with a cheap plastic doll. Haunting an elevator, of all places. But Danton'd started talking about his job at the law school book store and his asshole boss, then about a movie he wanted to see, then about how his sister was getting on his case about him not phoning their mother more often, and every time I opened my mouth I shut it again.

We'd been together eight months. No world's record, but still.

After he left, I lay in bed for a long time, thinking. Crap, if I'd wanted to—needed to—talk about it, I should've just started in. Danton was sweet and calm and sexy, but he wasn't a damn mind reader. Maybe he'd wanted to talk about it, too, but had been afraid to upset me, so kept chattering about inconsequential stuff. On top of it all, I was never going to figure out that tree problem in trans gen class, ever.

There was a dead kid in the elevator.

I think I fell asleep around four. And woke up around eight.

Without showering or even combing my hair—I barely grabbed the time to yank on yesterday's jeans and yesterday's Catatonic U t-shirt—I ran down to Mrs. Blomberg's apartment. Four flights.

She was up. Old people are like that. She was wearing a robe over a flowered nightgown, but as soon as she opened the door I smelled coffee and toast and eggs; she'd already had breakfast. Probably been awake since dawn.

She knew. As soon as she saw me standing in the hallway, breathing a little fast from the dash down the stairs, her face went pale; her faded blue eyes in their nests of wrinkles darted left and right, searching for escape. Her chin trembled.

She didn't let me in. We conducted the whole conversation with me standing in the corridor and her clinging white-knuckled to the door frame.

"Who is she?" My mouth was so dry the words came out in a croak.

Mrs. Blomberg shook her head.

"Who was she?"

I waited her out. I knew how to do that. I'd had lots of practice.

"It was a long time ago," she said at last. Her voice quavered. It usually did; she had Parkinson's or something, one of those trembling diseases. But this was different.

Mrs. Blomberg couldn't look me in the face.

"Tell me," I said.

"You weren't even born yet," and she did look at me then, a brief, bitter glance. "You weren't even born."

"Tell me." My pulse throbbed in my throat.

Mrs. Blomberg whispered, "She doesn't always . . . she isn't always in the elevator. Only once in a while. Years have gone by . . ."

I waited.

"She lived here. She died here. That's all I can say."

"Who killed her?"

Mrs. Blomberg flinched. "I don't know."

I saw something in her eyes then, something terrible.

"You do."

She shook her head, very hard.

"He still lives here, doesn't he?"

The old woman trembled like a leaf in a storm.

"How can you stand it?" I was mimicking Danton, automatically, almost unconsciously: voice low, modulated, even. The mask of calm.

"I've been here since 1960. I couldn't—I can't—there's nowhere—"

It took me a moment to get it. There was nowhere else she could afford.

"You all know, don't you? You all know who did it."

Mrs. Blomberg didn't answer.

"My god." My imitation of Danton cracked right down the middle.

"You don't understand. Kids like you, you can't understand."

"Dolly-fucking," I said, viciously. Venomously. "Dolly-fucking-*fucking*."

"It's not—I don't—"

"Has he done it again?" I shouted at her. Screamed, maybe. "Has the fucking bastard done it again? How many times? Is he still doing it?"

"I don't—I can't—" Mrs. Blomberg was shaking so hard she couldn't speak.

"Dolly-fucking." My stomach clenched; I came within a millisecond of puking right in the hallway. "Rent control. Fucking rent control?"

"Wait until you're old," she whispered.

"You didn't."

I spun on my heel, fury and grief and outrage and righteousness buoying me up, and stomped down the corridor. To the elevator.

I wanted to see her again, the little girl. Just at that moment there was nothing more I wanted in the world. This time I would embrace her, hug her, smooth her matted, filthy hair and tell her than it would all be okay, that there was no reason to be afraid any more, that somebody cared, that someone would help . . .

Of course the elevator was empty. It stayed empty. I got off on my floor, still feeling sick, still feeling furious, but . . . a little relieved.

The first thing I did after slamming into my apartment was phone Danton.

Woke him out of a sound sleep.

"Let's get a place together," I said.

It took a while to make him understand that I meant finding a place somewhere else, not me moving my stuff up to his apartment or him hauling his things down to mine, and not because he was muzzy from sleep. Danton came alert real fast after my first sentence. He just refused to grasp what I was saying. Or refused to admit that he grasped it. By the third or fourth go-round, my own mind was in a whirl. I was hardly making sense. I hadn't expected it would be so hard. That was maybe the most awful thing, how hard it was to talk to Danton. Because it shouldn't have been.

"I'm coming down," he said, after I just started crying and couldn't talk any more at all.

Shaking, hugging myself, my arms wrapped around my body like a little kid, I waited by the door. I opened it as soon as I heard his steps in the hall.

"I don't understand—" His first words, in that soft, controlled voice, and suddenly I was furious at him, at calm quiet Danton who had been so upset when he saw the dead girl in the elevator, but who didn't really care, not about her. *I could've strangled her*, he'd said.

"I can't stay here!" I yelled at him. "I can't live here. How can you?"

Danton shut my door. Carefully. Quietly. "Listen. You're worked up, but—yeah, it freaks me out, too, okay? A ghost, I mean, shit. But I've got a lease, Melanie. And so do you."

Lease?

I think I stared at Danton for a full minute. He was talking during that whole time, but I didn't register a single thing he said.

Then, though I'd already told him everything over the phone, I explained again what I'd dragged out of Mrs. Blomberg. That the man who'd killed—who'd abused and killed—who'd raped and killed the girl still lived in our building. That it most likely wasn't the first or the last time he'd done it. That he might still be doing it. One of our neighbors. One of my neighbors. One of his goddamn neighbors.

"You don't know that for sure," Danton said. "You don't know anything for sure."

I stopped listening again. A rush of ice water through my guts: Mr Dane? Mr. Myers? Mr. Biaggio? Who?

My teeth chattered. Danton didn't touch me. Didn't even try.

"What are you going to do the next time you're on the elevator and she shoves that doll in your face?"

Danton's lips twitched, skinning back from his teeth for a flicker of a second—his was of showing he was pissed. He took a long, steadying breath, and said, "I think I'm going to take the stairs from now on. Good exercise, you know," with a little laugh, as if it was a damn joke.

"Danton." One last time, I tried to make him understand. "Staying here means you think what happened was okay. Is okay. What happened to her," and I choked again, couldn't finish.

"Moving won't change the past," he said. That was the closest he came to acknowledging the ghost in the elevator as anything other than one of those inconveniences of city living that you learn to deal with and convince yourself to mostly ignore, like police sirens screaming away in the middle of the night, or garbage strikes.

Staying here makes us part of it, I wanted to say. I didn't. He wouldn't have heard me anyway.

I'd picked up my groceries, and I'd fled. Fleeing from her had been bad enough, but worse was that I'd grabbed my frigging shopping first.

It took me six weeks to find a new apartment. Danton called a few times. One of the last things he said to me was, "You're just running away. How does that help?"

I hated him for that.

I avoided my neighbors. Every one of them, men and women, old and young.

I saw the dead girl twice more before I moved.

The first time I was alone in the elevator. Same as before, I smelled her first. Rank, rotting, a garbage reek. Cold sweat slicked me. My knees did a funny little tremor-dance, totally beyond my control.

"Dolly-fucking," whispered, in a bare, sad thread of a voice.

Slowly I turned, very slowly, just enough to glimpse her out of the corner of my eye. The dead kid was crouched at the back of the elevator, against the wall, her eyes cast down and her face hidden by her filthy, matted hair. The doll dangled between her bent knees. The girl held it by the ankles, listlessly.

"You're not a dolly," I said. I don't know where the words came from; I don't know how my own voice stayed so calm.

The girl didn't look up, didn't reply, didn't do anything. When the elevator halted, I got off.

The second time, the last time, a bunch of old people were in the lift with me. Not Mrs. Blomberg, she wasn't there, but Mrs. Borda was, and Mrs. Golovin, and a couple of other old ladies, and Mr. Dane.

In the crowded elevator, the smell was even stronger. I wouldn't have guessed that was possible.

The others all pretended they didn't notice a thing. Mr. Dane stared at the floor buttons as they lit up and blinked out in sequence. One of the old women I couldn't put a name to continued chatting to Mrs. Golovin about the block party they were going to be holding next week.

"Dolly-fucking!" the dead kid screamed, her shrill voice piercing through my temples like an ice-cold needle.

Mrs. Golovin and the other woman kept talking.

Mr. Dane kept staring at the floor buttons.

The rest of them kept pretending as hard as they could that nothing unusual was happening.

"Dolly-fucking! Dolly-fucking!"

"Dolly-fucking," I said, swiveling around to look at each of them in turn, each and every damn one of them. None would meet my eyes.

"Dolly-fucking!" the dead girl screamed, and "Dolly-fucking," I repeated, each time she screamed it.

Over and over.

Until the elevator stopped on my floor.

I stepped out.

"Dolly-fucking!" the kid shrieked.

"Dolly-fucking," I said, low and slow and even, as the elevator doors slid shut.

A few days later I finally found a place I could afford; I slapped down first-and-last month and the security deposit with lightning speed, called a moving company, got my stuff boxed and out.

Something . . . the embers of desire, the remnant of an illusion, a last hope . . . made me phone Danton before I left for good.

He didn't pick up.

He had an answering machine which always clicked on after the fourth ring, but he must've disconnected it. The phone rang and rang, until finally I hung up.

I never saw Danton again.

I've never seen a ghost again, either. But I still wonder sometimes which of us was more wrong, Danton who stayed, or me who ran away so I wouldn't have to think about the dead girl and the man who dolly-fucked her, about all the men who dolly-fuck, every single day for the rest of my life.

MATTERS OF FAMILY

GARY A. BRAUNBECK

"Man has places in his heart which do not yet exist, and into them enters suffering, in order that they may have existence."

—Leon Bloy

Albert stared out the window and watched the world melt under the weight of rain. Small sections of tree bark slid off a stump and sank into the mud, all of it flowing toward the fence where it picked up a few thin branches of shrubbery that looked like twisted arms reaching, a form too much like the misshapen thing on the bed behind him; silent, unmoving, his responsibility now.

"Did she give you any . . . trouble?" he asked.

"None," replied Fran. He turned toward her voice, searching through the gloom for some echo he expected to take form over his head. Beyond the bed, down near the corner of the door, a small blue nightlight glowed. It was shaped like an annoying cartoon character from Saturday morning television. He almost thought the voice had come from its mouth.

"Will you . . . um, is there anything you need?" Fran asked.

"Not that I can think of. Has she been . . . did she go to the bathroom?" He blinked, cursing himself for phrasing it that way. *Of course she didn't go to the bathroom, you idiot. In order to do that she'd have to be able to stand, know where it was, and walk there on her own power. What you really want to know is did she pee or shit herself, and did Fran change the diaper?*

"Yes," replied Fran. "She's all taken care of for the night."

Albert lit a cigarette, took a deep drag, watched as the blue-tinted smoke curled toward the ceiling. He remembered the way his mother had always gotten angry at having to change the diaper twice, sometimes three times an hour; she always rolled her eyes toward the ceiling, as if expecting something to drift down and spare her the task. Of course, that was always the way around the house, at least when he lived here; there was really nothing wrong with Suzanne, she was just a VERY ILL little girl, a girl who would someday GET BETTER, a SICKLY child who, with time, patience, and caring, would be UP an AT 'EM in no time, just you watch.

"I hope you don't mind my asking," said Fran, "but, well . . . how was . . . ?"

"The turnout? A lot of people came. I hadn't realized that Mom and Dad had so many friends." Something shifted within the blue cartoon glow, blocking the tail of his smoke snake. He took another drag as the rain drummed impatient fingers along the metal gutter. Small strands of smoke twisted before his face: he'd just walked into a spider's web, and Fran, with a wave of her hand, swept the web up toward the ceiling before he became entangled.

"May I fix you some coffee?" she said. "Maybe something to eat?"

"Some hot tea might be nice." His eyes were fixed on the bed and the thing lying upon it. He remembered that he'd known it. It was his sister. It had a name. Suzanne, wasn't it?

Her eyes were glossy, blank, open.

Staring toward the ceiling like Mother so often did. *Had.*

Somewhere heavy streams of water and mud were pulsing toward the open graves, pouring over the edges, slipping down, pools slowly rising, drowning the caskets. But then Mom and Dad were used to that; they'd drowned once already. Dad and his little boat. Mom hadn't wanted to go out with him that day, the weather looked too unstable, but Dad was never one to let something like that stop him from enjoying the open sea and—

"Come on," said Fran, taking his hand. Before he left he turned once more toward his sister. She, also, was tinted in cartoon blue. Had he not known better, he would have thought she was suffocating. And what if she were? Would she even realize it? What could he do?

He could close the door, pretending not to notice.

Which is what he did.

The brightness of the kitchen's overhead light was too much for him; he flipped the switch and dropped the room into a greyness like the brief flashes one might see behind closed eyes.

Fran prepared the tea, then sat across from him as he sipped. She'd made it too hot.

"What are you going to do with her?" she said.

"Hell if I know. Maybe put her in some kind of home. I don't know the first thing about how to take care of a . . . of her." He set his cup down and looked at Fran. "She always scared me, even when I was a kid."

"You mean she's . . . older than you?"

"She's thirty-one. She stopped growing by the time I was eleven. All the doctors expected her to die before she turned eighteen. Mom never wanted to put her away; she thought it was cruel."

"And your father?"

"He never talked about it much. I never saw him go into her room, ever, except for this one night. I got up, it was about, oh, three in the morning and I saw him at the foot of the stairs. He was standing at her door, staring in. Then he looked around, took this real deep breath, and went in so . . . quickly. Like he'd been doing it for a long time and hadn't gotten caught. I remember I tiptoed down and stood by the door, listening.

"He *read* to her, as if he couldn't believe that she couldn't . . .

"It was pretty strange. I tried, I really tried to love her. I knew that I should've because she was my sister; she came from the same part of Mom and Dad that I did, so we were both kind of . . . *the same* in that way, you know? No one ever mentioned putting her away when there were other people around. It was one of our private things, one of those matters of family that never left the house under any circumstances." He sipped his tea again; the temperature was just right.

"I even tried reading to her one night, but it got to the point where my voice sounded like it was being sucked into the walls. She never so much as blinked. All I ever wanted from her was just some kind of *reaction*, something that would tell me I was getting through. And I remember that night when I listened to Dad reading to her, I *swear* she giggled. I dunno, though; maybe it was just wishful thinking."

"Would you like me to hang around for a while? I can, you know. Jim's with the kids and he's not expecting me home at any certain time."

He looked through the greyness at Fran's eyes. Kind eyes. He wondered why he hadn't snatched her up when he had the chance.

"Probably wouldn't be the best idea," he said. "I make no guarantees that I'd behave myself." There was a brief glint of something that might have been mischief in her eyes, and he wondered if she really loved her husband and children or if—like him—she'd awakened one morning and found her body wrapped so tightly in family matters that backing out was impossible. As he reached over and took her hand, he wondered if love within a family—or between a man and a woman, for that matter—took a back seat to necessity, a nagging feeling that you didn't love so much because you wanted to, but because you felt obligated to. And what then? Easy: the happiness and welfare of those you loved, things you once vowed to hold sacred, became less a loving task and more a burden you no longer wished to bear, draping its arms around your neck like a child wanting to ride piggy-back, pulling in, slowly cutting off your breath. But you couldn't just cast it away, this burdensome child, because you were all it had, like it or not. Everything became secondary to the burden of that obligation. Even love.

"Little Miss Muffet," he said.

"*What?*" said Fran, the word a half-laugh.

"Little Miss Muffet. Dad was reading that to her. I remember I heard her giggle at the part about the spider." He watched the thin streams of steam rise from the tea and vanish into the greyness, taking on no certain shape before it dissolved.

A sound came from the back of the house. A child-sound. Fran didn't seem to notice.

"I don't know what made me think of that," he said, lighting another cigarette, wondering if Fran would wave her hand before the strings of smoke entangled his neck and choked him to death. He wondered how blue his face would get before he lost consciousness—or did suffocation victims die that way, their features twisted and discolored forever?

He glanced at Fran through the sputtering flame of his lighter.

She was looking at the ceiling.

Fran kissed him when she left, a kiss that was a little too friendly and went on a little too long. She promised to call him in the morning and come over to help him with Suzanne if he wanted. He held her hand for a moment, gently brushing his fingertips over her palm once so soft and now showing signs of hardness, dryness brought on from washing too many dishes, mending too many socks, changing too many diapers. As he watched her dash out toward her car, he saw—through the droplets of rain that seemed to shimmer from within like a candle flame—what would become of her, what became of all women he'd known who chose the life of wife and mother; a young woman so vibrant and trim and lovely, going happily away promising to return home one day a woman of the world, waving with hands that always became calloused, running on legs that always grew too heavy, smiling a smile that always grew tired, uncertain and finally false—all this he saw ignite around her in brief shimmerings of rain. She'd kissed him as a young woman, smiled at him from the steps middle-aged, and climbed into her car an overweight, dreamless matron, driving off toward a marriage that would one day seem futile, trap-like, if not outright parasitic.

He closed the door on this image and shook his head.

Get a drink. Something stronger than tea.

Four drinks and six cigarettes later, he opened the door to his sister's room and stared at her. She was still breathing, Cartoon Blue hadn't done her in yet. He walked in, closed the door, and pulled up a chair. He downed what was left in the glass, sat next to her.

"Why didn't you ever giggle for me?" he said, watching the ash of his cigarette grow long. "Why couldn't you have given me just one lousy little response?" He watched as the ash fell off, just missing the covers.

An idea came to him.

"I could do it, you know? Just blow on the cherry until it's real hot, lay it next to your pillow and leave, drink a little more. I might go to court, but I'd never do any time. A young man—well, not old anyway—his parents not ten hours in their graves, saddled with the responsibility of caring for a . . . his sister, drinks a bit too much to ease the day, falls asleep with the cigarette, and—"

The holes in that story began presenting themselves to him with loud and annoying fanfare.

It wasn't in him.

But Suzanne frightened him; worse than anything he'd ever known.

He winced, knowing how ashamed his father would be were he still alive and knew the horrid thoughts his son had been having.

"Do you miss them?" he whispered to the still form. "Were you ever even aware they were here?"

The smoke danced about the ceiling, jumping around like water on a hot griddle. Then it once again began to take form.

"Little Miss Muffet sat on her tuffet," he said.

—*wagon wheel the smoke looks like a wagon wheel don't it Sis?*

" . . . eating her curds and whey . . ."

—*what the hell is whey I never ate that crap and goddamn boy no son of mine would ever think something like that you ought to be ashamed she knows that you're around she's your sister and she loves you just like your mother and me—*

" . . . along came a spider . . ."

A sound from within the pillow. No. On the pillow.

He leaned in close.

Her breathing, soft, smooth, constant, broken by a slight sound like a plump bug being squashed—

A tiny, almost imperceptible giggle.

He crushed the cigarette out in his hand, grinding in the hot ash.

"I feel so much better," he said, then leaned in and kissed her on the forehead. Her face felt funny to him, wider than he remembered. Although Cartoon Blue gave off some light, it was not enough to make out her features. He cupped both his hands on the sides of her face, gently pushing back her hair. His fingers felt where her left ear *should have* been, only there was something *hard* there, something sticking out. He took a breath, slowly turning her head so as not to put a strain on her throat—*God knows we don't want anything to happen to her breathing*—and bent down, blinking his eyes until he was sure his vision was clear. He ran his fingers down her cheek to where the side of her neck *should have* been, but there were pink wet lips there. He stood back to look. It seemed so natural to him that the two of them should be together like this, and which, *you might ask yourself,* is the real face and which is the Halloween mask that has slid to one side?

A small laugh escaped him.

Suzanne's face lay toward Cartoon Blue.

His mother's face lay staring up at him.

"I wondered how long it would take," he said to her.

"You have to be good," said his mother from the side of Suzanne's head. "You have to help us, Albert. Take care of us."

"I always did, Mom."

"Yes, honey, that you did." Her eyes darted up to a string of Suzanne's hair. "Please cover me back up. I don't want to frighten Fran when she comes back."

"I will. It's good to see you again, Mom."

"Goodnight, Albert."

He brushed the hair down, taking one last look into his mother's eyes, now only the briefest of glimmering stars behind the nightclouds of Suzanne's hair. "Goodnight, Mom."

He then turned his sister's face back around and again kissed her on the forehead. "They never could let go of you," he said. He rose, went to the kitchen, poured another drink, stared at the clock.

It was almost ten p.m.

He checked her again at midnight, his chest burning from booze and cigarettes.

Dad was back now, a second mask on the other side of Suzanne's head, but he was sleeping; Albert new that one did not disturb his father's sleep for any reason. They'd talk in the morning, like they always had. *Did.*

Back to the kitchen now where his parents sat waiting for him, their faces gone and in their place a smooth sheet of sallow flesh. They reminded him of those "Any Face You Want" dolls he'd had as a child, dolls that were dressed like soldiers or policemen and had nothing for a face, but that was all right because they came with a pen that could draw in four erasable colors so you could draw whatever face you wanted with whatever expression you chose.

He looked at how they sat.

Dad-doll sat at the kitchen table, hands folded together as if in prayer, a cup of cold coffee before him. Albert remembered many nights of seeing his father this way alone, sitting in the dark, lost in deep concern over his family, finances, or where his younger dreams had gone once the marriage vows had been taken.

That's how I remember you, Dad. So quiet, so serious. You never once smiled, not that I saw. I always meant to ask you why.

Mom-doll was over in the living room, sitting in her favorite chair with a cup of tea and a sandwich on her lap, waiting for a late night re-run of a once popular hospital drama that had a cute young doctor. It was always the high point of her day. Albert waited for her to turn toward him and ask if he'd like to join her, she had no company at night and watching the show was so much better if you—

But she had no mouth to speak with. Or eyes to see. Still she waited for the show to start.

And Albert had no four-color pen with erasable ink.

Why these? he thought.

Why, of all the memories you could have left me, did you choose these? I remember these so well, Mom and Dad, because, to me, they *were* you. If all images and memories of you were to be sucked out of my brain, these would be the ones too powerful ever to leave me.

And they were also the worst. Because he'd know at these times his parents gave everything second place to obligation. And were alone and lonely because of it. Helpless and entangled and choking and nailed down to a life and family, neither of which had turned out as they'd hoped.

He turned away, grabbed the bottle of scotch and a fresh pack of cigarettes, and went to his old bedroom in the back. It was just as he'd left it—sparse. A bed, a dresser, a chair, a desk, and nothing more. He kept a makeshift work space here, just in case his own apartment grew too quiet some night. He could always come back here.

Back to the family.

And matters of.

The burning in his chest grew worse over the next four hours, but he kept smoking one cigarette after another, at one point discovering that he had five going at the same time.

Around four-thirty in the morning he heard another child-sound from Suzanne's room. He crept slowly toward the door, pressed his ear against it.

She was giggling.

" . . . and frightened Miss Muffet away," came the dull echo of his father's voice, speaking in rhythm with the drumming fingers of rain on the roof. A silent flash of lightning, raindrops into candle flames and Dad began reciting another, different verse.

"You never read stories to me," whispered Albert to the door. "I always wanted you to, but you never did."

He turned and went back to his drink, to his cigarettes. He tried to fall asleep, but the constant murmuring of their voices kept him around. At five he picked up the phone. Dialed. Listened as the phone buzzed, buzzed, buzzed into a click and then a hiss and then—

" . . . lo?" The voice was soft, thick with sleep

"Fran?"

The voice coughed, cleared its throat. "Albert? That you?"

"Yeah, Jim. Sorry to wake you." There was the sound of sheets rustling. Whispering. He closed his eyes, imagining what Jim had been doing to Fran before sleep took them away to a false safety and security. The things. Warm and moist.

Fran, at last.

"Albert? Is everything all right?"

I should've snatched you up when I had the chance. "I didn't mean to wake you, Fran. I'm sorry."

"Don't apologize. What is it? You okay?"

You'd never have let me come back here. "Could you . . . come back?"

"Is there something wrong with Suzanne?"

"Sort of. She won't stop giggling."

" . . . what?"

I never would have felt so goddamn responsible. "It's not so much . . . so much her, though." The smoke of his new cigarette blew up, scattered, pulled back, webbing, webbing, coming toward him— "It's Mom and Dad, they're keeping her awake."

Silence from the other end; the web kept coming and Fran wasn't here to wave it away . . .

" . . . drunk?"

"Maybe a little," said Albert.

"I knew I should've stayed."

Would you have let me be warm and moist with you like Jim? "I think they're mad at me. They didn't give me any pen to draw . . . their faces with."

"I'll be over in a few minutes. You just stay put and don't drink any more, all right?"

" . . . sucked it all out, all of them but those two . . . don't know why . . ." He felt weak, as if his limbs were wrapped in rope.

The smoke-web widened.

The giggling grew louder.

He didn't even hear Fran hang up. He kept talking into the receiver.

" . . . always wanted to help them out, you know . . . but I never counted on having to run their whole lives . . . poor little thing, I should've been more . . . love her, really I did because maybe she understands love, maybe, and . . ."

Click. Squeak.

Suzanne's door opened.

Giggling.

He kept talking.

"Was never really a part of things . . . wanted to be, though. The thing is that I never really tried. I just worried about it too much . . ." He didn't realize that he'd begun weeping. He took another drag, another drink. The burning grew worse, snaking through him. He looked up at the ceiling. Something dangled there, thin, vein-like, rough-looking . . . maybe . . . hairy . . . ?

" . . . never read to me. I always wondered why. He always worried so much about things . . ."

Giggling. A brushing of something against his leg.

He leaned back, closed his eyes, let the receiver drop.

Weight shifted around him; he felt arms, legs, lips touching against his cheek, words whispered, embraces, warm, so many hands, long, thin, weak, bumpy, strong, twisted . . .

. . . he opened his eyes and saw the web descend toward him.

Pounding, pounding . . . he thought maybe in his head.

No, the door.

Fran. She'd wave it away, save him from being strangled by Cartoon Blue.

He started to move from the chair, found that he was already standing.

Looking back where he sat, the Albert-doll, no face, no tears, only the cigarette ash on his pant leg, the cherry growing brighter, falling off, flames licking at his clothes like the tongue of a lover . . .

He moved toward the door as his father spoke.

"Your sister wants you to read to her, Albert. Would you like that? I'll read to you, too, if you'd like. Seems the least I can do."

"Let's all read to her," said Mom.

"Yeah," said Albert. "That would be nice."

Suzanne giggled.

It was good for them to be together like this.

Behind him, the Albert-doll was sitting there, holding hands with Mom-doll and Dad-doll, all of them seeming so happy, burning away as the smoke-web wrapped around them, arms twisting together, legs sticking out like—

Mother's voice: "*Little Miss Muffet sat on her tuffet . . .*"

Flash of lightning and Albert saw their reflection in the mirror, so clear, turning full circle so each could get a good look at the face—

Father now: "*. . . eating her curds and whey . . .*"

The flames spit up higher and Albert knew he'd let the cigarette drop for a reason, because they needed the web, yes they did, there was no other way for them to entangle, and entanglement was the only action left them . . .

. . . poundpoundpoundpound . . .

"Albert!" Fran's voice. She sounded so worried. *No need to worry now, Fran, everything's fine, we've settled our private family matters.*

"*. . . along came a spider . . . ,*" said Albert, reaching for the door, turning the knob.

"*. . . and sat down beside her . . . ,*" said all of them.

Freed, the door swung open.

Pleased, Suzanne giggled.

Completed, the web offered shelter.

Scuttling around on the arms and legs, twisting and smiling, Albert and his family looked up.

Given a clear look by the pouring firedrops, Fran began screaming.

—for Charles L. Grant

THERE THE GREAT CITY STANDS

CERI JORDAN

There is a city. A odd, unfettered city where hawkers coax gullible courting couples with dishes of crisp sweetmeats and handfuls of yellow daisies under a blue-white sun; self-proclaimed prophets rant at lazy merchants in courtyards full of lime trees or are obscenely mocked by the boy-whores on the bath-house steps; poets hold drunken rhyming contests at midnight on the cracked ochre paving stones of Sorrell Matin, while the bells toll a passing at the plague hospital and the benevolent stars look down.

I have spent all my life trying to get there.

I was born a launderess' daughter in the fierce raw desolation of an Eastern market town that needs no name because all others are identical to it. Though I left young, to escape my mother's fate—red rheumatic knuckles, the thickening neck and downcast, sour eyes of a coal-pony, watching the young women in the windswept square as if puzzled that she was no longer one of them—I remember it sometimes with ambivalent affection.

In the spring there would be a fair, and boats came up the river with sugared almonds and bolts of silk in colours we had never even imagined: we crept shyly to finger them, to reassure ourselves that they were real, and the fat asthmatic traders would chase us away wailing about damage to their merchandise. The very word was marvellous to us; merchandise, a word of distant places, unimagined lives. No merchandise here: only skinny sheep and clay and the eternal undiminishing heaps of coal awaiting barges, raven against the shifting muted browns of the moorland.

Autumn, the streets scoured by an east wind and the rowans aflame in the magistrate's garden; the town festival. The chief clerk's daughter read her own execrable poetry, standing on a dais decorated with green ribbons under the long-rusted clock tower, and the magistrate made long and vaguely incoherent speeches about the spirit of the people, while adults and children alike shuffled and fidgeted, waiting for the real business of the afternoon to begin. The feasting, and the Stum Fight, where the young men were set to chase a year-old sow around the fenced-off streets; he who caught it would keep it, and since a sow made a fair bride-price in those days, the struggle was fierce and dirty, and the losers returned sheepishly rubbing their bloodied noses and shrugging apologies to girls haughty with disappointment.

The next morning the slaughtering of meat for the winter would begin: slaughterhouse men came up on a barge from Pinna, and we all ran to watch their gleaming knives flicker and scythe in the dull sulphurous light reflecting from the river, the goats' spindly legs skidding out from under them as steel flashed brilliant and blood fountained in the still air.

When at last I left for Locutrix, it was on the same barge as the returning slaughtermen, and seeing my skinny arms and coarse practical clothes, they smiled and looked quickly away.

It is a large city, Locutrix, centre of a salvage glass trade, and it takes itself seriously. It has a music-house where bewigged moribund men play great tragedies, and draughty halls where expressive dancers entertain smallholders squandering their year's savings on "a week in the city," returning chastened, aching, and clutching charms against the pox. Pot-houses serving the latest fashionable concoctions, too, each with its own unofficial school of poets and dilettantes. For a penny, girls lounging in the orphanage courtyard will tell you where to find whichever wit or epigrammist you most admire; for eightpence they will track him down for you, scuttling among the crowded streets exchanging sightings, *Mima Casquen drinks herself to death under the faded sign of the Cheap Refection; Lithia regales a crowd on the heath with an improvised saga three hundred lines long and still growing, hurry or we'll miss it . . .*

I grew a little taller, filled out, gained by that peculiar combination of persistence and chance employment writing for a broadsheet, wrote satires that the music-house performed to acclaim and empty seats, built up my own small following, took lovers, vile alcohols, and rest-cures.

But I still had not found my city.

What is it I seek, you ask? Some child's fantasy, where the sun always shines and there are no beggars or thieves or raised voices to spoil my utopia? I began to suspect it was; and then I saw.

Returning late from an assignation at the bath-house that is better forgotten, I went down an alley that I had not noticed before, dark and smelling of piss, a marital squabble audible behind the coloured glass of a high window as I passed. When I emerged, the lamps hung in the trees were the exact colour of sunset light, beautiful and sad: the streets were golden under its caress, and a group of dancers were performing an oddly graceful entertainment on a raised piazza for a nobleman I did not recognise.

I stared.

The nobleman's entourage swirled and strutted in their peacock finery, raising goblets of sparkling wine to the light, cheering the dancers, paying court to them as they stumbled off the stage, kissing their puffy hands and tweaking playfully at already scanty costumes. I stepped forward into the lamplight –

I stood alone on the grey expanse of Maundy, torn playhouse posters flapping in the breeze.

"Why..?" I said aloud, and my words rang back at me from the metal warehouses, tinny and muffled: "Why me?"

In the alley opposite, someone laughed hoarsely and scuttled away.

I continued to live: interviewed the periwigged tragedians and found them, apart from their roles, ill-informed and tiresome; wrote a satire which the chief magistrate banned, then blackmailed him into compensating me for the financial loss; scandalised the merchant classes by conducting a tempestuous and ridiculously public affair with the senior ballerina of the music-house . . .

Again and again, I found myself upon streets I did not know, looking upon people like none I had ever imagined. Crossing the river bridge at dawn I saw a crowd jeering a man mounting the gallows; when the hangman jerked the steps away they fell instantly silent, watching the pitiful convulsions intently, as if memorising them. By the time I passed behind the high hedge onto the heath, there was neither crowd nor gallows, only the stamp and scurry of rabbits in a cold mist.

I hummed a tune I heard coming from a playhouse that did not exist to Scarba, music master of the Palace of Virtue and Beauty, and he offered me two percent of the profits if I would let him use it for a display; I agreed, and attended it, ill at ease in the perfumed guest-box being gaped at by the groundlings. The girls postured and wriggled without enthusiasm or grace, and the tune did not seem quite the same; whining, cruder, coarser. I suspected I had misheard it anyway. The crowds cheered with their normal lazy inattention and settled back to wait for the more explicit material. I left.

Walking home, I passed boys burning a effigy of a dragon that they had somehow managed to float on the musty pond above the municipal court. They had stuffed its slack mouth with firecrackers and were hesitantly daring one another to stand closer, closer—

Hearing no explosion, I glanced back. The waters of the pond were smooth and faintly luminous with algae, and the boys were no longer there. Instead, an old woman in a mud-spattered yellow silk gown was examining the damp compacted earth with dissatisfaction. "It leaks through," she said loudly, to no one in particular. "Do what you please, it will leak through —"

"What will?"

She turned unsteadily, regarded me with her head cocked to one side like a bird.

"The city. You're talking about the city?"

"What would you know about it if I were, eh?"

I spread my hands wide in a pacifying gesture, lest she feared I was a thief or a gang-leader, and said slowly and distinctly, "I wish to go to the city. That city, you understand."

"Griphos Tower!" she said abruptly, with a stale, venomous grin. "Noon tomorrow."

Fool that I am, I let her go.

I waited all afternoon at Griphos Tower, under the gaze of the priests bustling about the Shrine of the Logarithm—a heap of papers sealed behind glass, so old that the necessary rituals are lost and the priests invent their own showy observances and vie with one another in self-abasement—but she did not come. Infuriated, I collected my two percent from Scarba and drank myself into a stupor in the filthy ale-houses along the river, waking before dawn with my head in a puddle and the contents of my pockets gone.

Then I saw her again.

She was vanishing into the side door of one of the irregular little houses along Tritium Brook, where in the summer mercenaries loiter for hire and shy willowy girls hang out of the window and fantasise.

Among the jutting porches and leaning walls it took me a moment to find the right door: when I pushed it, it swung gently open, and her quick footsteps scuffled on the narrow stairway above my head.

I considered calling up to her, unsure whether that would frighten her more; began to climb. Dust lay thick all the way up, undisturbed by her passing. I kicked in the locked door on the final landing, and she sat there, holding a white pigeon in her hands, speaking soothingly to it, stroking its head with the ball of her thumb. Without looking up she said, "You should not be here."

"You promised me a way to the city."

"I promised nothing."

Strictly, of course, that was absolutely correct; but it angered me all the more, and I strode across the tiny garret room, gagging on the stink of rotting leaves, and seized her by the arm. "The city. Tell me, and tell me now."

"Be sure," she said, "that what you wish is what you want—"

"I don't want philosophy, I want answers!"

She laughed, but seeing my expression nodded quickly. "Wait. It is not yet time."

"For what?"

"Watch the bird," she murmured, looking quickly at the window, where the first faint glimpse of the rising sun bled yellow through dirty glass, "the bird is the key, careful or it will escape—"

I released her arm, and she pressed the bird close to her cheek, making thin soothing noises to it. When she released it, it rose with a peculiar motion of its wings, eyes glassy, astonished, flew at the closed window, into the glare: flaring and brightening now, the colour of blood, dazzling . . .

"Follow if you can!" the old woman sneered, and darted forward into the blazing sun.

I hurled myself after her.

For a moment after regaining consciousness, I could not remember what had happened. Then, sitting up, I saw her running away up a long street between lime trees, where tall women in peculiar slim gowns examined one another's fans with curious disinterest. The pavements were golden, the minarets silver and ultramarine, the air full of the sound of tiny crystal bells.

The city.

So I came here.

I was quite the fashion, for a time; the coy women and the slender perfect gentlemen flocked to the playhouse and the gin parlours to see the woman from another world, and gave generous gifts with the carelessness of the totally unconcerned. I sat for several portraits, and etchings of me in heroic poses were circulated in literary circles; there were interviews and books and metaphysical speculations and lazily intrigued would-be seducers of both sexes –

It passed, of course.

I have tried to write, but while the broadsheets purchase occasional pieces for their novelty value, my work is regarded with the startled, amused contempt they would apply to a dancing pig or a talking dog. I would not mind, but I read their work, and by comparison they are right.

I wear clothes by the finest tailors, and on me they look slovenly and misshapen. I cannot sing the songs they write. I find the footwear impractical, the exquisite symmetrical houses too perfect, even the cutlery fussy and fragile. I am an ape in a world of men.

It is a terrible thing, to be the only imperfection in Utopia.

I took to searching the swirling, smiling crowds for the source of my humiliation.

And last night at last I found her, the old woman, kneeling on the cobbles humming to herself as blue fire played across the stones, smiling as an idiot might smile at some secret inward jest.

She did not hear me approach; seizing the shotten fabric of her filthy gown, I pulled her back into the alley and garrotted her. She struggled, briefly; bony fingers clutching, heart fluttering like a bird. Her eyes bulged, her tongue hung slack from her rotten mouth: she looked absurd. I propped her in an immaculate doorway and left her there.

Today, in the gleaming sunlit squares and among the delightfully gaudy market stalls, they speak of her death in hushed tones. They say she was a powerful figure here; not politically, for they do not seem to understand the term, but spiritually, mystically. They say that without her the city may cease to exist.

Indeed, in the eastern quarter the sun already glares balefully through a thick blue fog, and there are rumours of pointless quarrels and strange secret revenges. A dog was found impaled upon the railings at Rutile Corner at dawn, they say, and the lake waters have turned to blood. A few brave souls are thought to be leaving the city, forcing the unfrequented gates and stumbling out into the thin misty sunlight beyond. But most are content simply to stand and wait. After all, they say, with bitter little smiles, where is there to go?

NIGHT WINDOW

MARC LECARD

The motel sign featured a large, curving, pulsating palm tree outlined in neon green and yellow; the motel called itself, of course, "The Palms." Deborah stared at the sign's reflection, and the reflection of red taillights in the street beyond, in the glass of the night window for a few moments, pulling herself together, getting ready for work. Then, taking a breath and holding it, she tapped on the glass as she had been taught to do: a quick, complicated rhythmic series, pads and clicks and paradiddles. It had taken her weeks to learn the pattern; now it came effortlessly.

Waiting for the night manager to come and give her the meeting for the night, she stared blankly through the paranoid schematics of the chicken wire embedded in the thick glass. The room beyond, scarcely an arm's length across, seemed like a sound studio in hell, painted dull beige, furnished only with a metal chair, floor lamp, and built-in desk.

The door in the far wall, painted the same stale, band-aid color, suddenly cracked open, and the manager came into the night room. He looked at her expressionlessly. His swift and angular movements disturbed her at some visceral, barely conscious level. She was used to this feeling by now, aware of the reasons for it, and for why she, of all people, should get over them. She fought down her loathing, from a sense of duty. "He can't help what he is," she told herself, "any more than you can."

Wordlessly, the manager slid a key through the slot at the bottom of the window. Deborah picked it up in silence, without reading the room number on the round plastic tag, and walked away.

It was always the same, for as long as she'd been working for them. How long? God, nearly five years now, since she'd passed the tests. Not that she had known they were tests at the time. I passed, she thought, because I didn't care. I didn't care at all about anything. No matter what weird shit they threw at me, I didn't get upset, because I really didn't care. At least it had felt like not caring at the time. Now she realized that all that time she had been wanting to die.

It was good to be beyond that, at least.

Sometimes you look for work, and sometimes it finds you. A teacher at the night school she went to for a while had suggested a new line of work for Deborah; he had been her first customer. A call girl, a courtesan, a prostitute: whatever. She had never walked the streets, though. Her clients had always come to her; that was a point of pride. She worked by herself, for herself. Word got around, people came to her. She'd done well, put some money away, made some good investments. One of her regulars gave her some good advice, worth far more than her fee. She used to dream of the time when she could give up turning tricks, and just groom her portfolio for a while.

Everything was different now, though. She would keep coming to the night window.

She wondered why they had chosen her, out of all the working women in the city, what it was about her that had led them to believe she would pass the tests and come to them. It occurred to her that they must have watched her sometimes, when she was at home, alone, or with other clients. Perhaps they still did. Some of her other clients were probably spies for them. It seemed likely. Fair, even. But no longer necessary. Still, it was like them to overdo caution and suspicion.

She read the room number by the overhead light in the parking lot, and walked slowly toward the rear stairs. The motel had doggedly carried out the tropical motif suggested by its name, with cast-iron palm-tree cutouts supporting the rails of the staircase and wrap-around balcony and the stucco walls painted in pastel shades, faded and stained by the cold foggy nights of the city.

The door was very slightly ajar, as always. She pushed it open slowly, so as not to startle whoever was inside.

He looked up expectantly as she came in. He sat quietly on one of the room's double beds, hands folded and hanging between his sharp-boned knees, silhouetted in the dim lamplight behind him so that she couldn't make out his features. Not that he would look much different from the others; all the faces ran into one generic mask, worn permanently. Only she, of all people, ever got to look beneath that mask.

It was truly a privilege, she realized that now. One not accorded to many.

She slid into the room and closed the door softly behind her. The first moments were always awkward. She supposed it was something like stagefright, something you never really got over, just learned to compensate for.

Her impulse was always to smile, to make small talk, to put them at ease. This was wasted, she knew that. Instead, she walked quickly to the side of the bed, bent forward, and ran her hands down the man's face and body, with a quick, light drumming of her fingers. She pressed her forehead against his. He responded wordlessly; she felt him mold to her, felt his excitement, his tension, his ardor.

At first it had been difficult, even after passing the tests. She had made mistakes, done things that should not have been done, or, what was as bad, done them in the incorrect sequence. But by this time she had the moves down cold, could do them in her sleep.

She stepped back from him, smiling in spite of herself—she knew it made no difference either way—and began to undress. The man undressed also. As always, she left most of her clothing on, as per the agreement, taking off only as much as necessary. It was easier for her that way, and seemed to make no difference to the clients.

The worst thing she had ever done wrong was not to clean up afterwards. Leaving things behind, that was the great sin. She supposed the risk of discovery was the most frightening thing to them. That they should be found out, at last, after all this time, after centuries of care and concealment. The worst thing.

That time, the first and last time she had forgotten, the night manager had been furious with her. He had become extremely disturbed, as much terrified as angry, scurrying around the seedy room in a frenzy, sweeping up the pale leafy fragments, spilling them, sweeping them up again. It had been an appalling spectacle. Looking at him hunched over the desk, reaching for a key on its plastic tag, thin, intense, focused on some inner broadcast, it was difficult to imagine the night manager losing his self-control. Without fully understanding it, Deborah had begun to share his terror. After that, she was always very careful to clean up afterward. She could still see and hear him, carefully searching the floor and the bedclothes with prying eyes that missed nothing, however small, all the while lecturing her in his tight, quiet voice, telling her the same thing over and over again, in slightly different forms:

Forget nothing. Leave nothing behind. Nothing, ever, ever. Nothing.

She had been perfect since that night.

The client had not spoken; they seldom did. But now he began to vocalize, a strange, harsh series of sounds, scrapings and raspings and clickings, sounds that seemed below speech, but that possessed a certain organization. A form. After all these years, these many nights, Deborah felt she was close to understanding what was being said.

It was almost time. She could feel him inside her, long and thin, probing, thrusting blindly, with surprising rapidity.

He was done. She felt a collapse, felt him cling to her, quivering, felt the appeal in his vibrating body. His need.

It was time.

Slowly, carefully, she brought her hands up to his neck. He bowed his head, trembling, waiting, wanting. How did it feel for them? she wondered, not for the first or the last time.

Digging in with her nails, she peeled back a long section of skin, pulling it up and off in a long, smooth motion. As the skin peeled off, it narrowed down, finally breaking free. Letting the fragment drop to the floor, she began again.

This part had been so hard, the first time, she had almost run from the room. Knowing them better now, she realized that such a move would have been instantly fatal.

It was like skinning a chicken; like undressing a child; like taking off your stockings. It was like nothing she had ever done.

Slowly and deliberately, she stripped off every bit of skin.

When she had finished, the carapace now exposed gleamed dully in the dim motel light. The chiton had a greenish tinge, fading to a tobacco brown at the extremities. A second pair of limbs, halfway down the long thin body of the creature, hung useless, atrophied, she supposed, from the long concealment and disuse.

With only the slightest hesitation, she leaned forward and bit into the smooth, brittle covering where the neck met the thorax.

The client trembled, and clung to her. He wants this, she marveled to herself, amazed and awed as always. This is what he wants me to do. She bit down harder, breaking off a large piece. It was both brittle and chewy, something like St. John's bread, a flexible, edible pod-skin. The fluids within—a greenish ichor—ran out; she drank them.

Slowly she consumed him, entirely.

At first she had thought that after all life had obviously left she could stop. The night manager had let her know, in no uncertain terms, that this was incorrect. All had to be consumed. It was more than fear of discovery, she thought now. This was sacrament, high office, and must be performed fully.

At first, she had worried that she couldn't possibly finish, that she simply hadn't the physical capacity. But, strangely, she had had no trouble, ever. Afterwards there was no unpleasant feeling of fullness; rather, an energizing. It had been a long time since she had felt happiness, but in her memory it felt like this.

And the taste—the taste—was overwhelming. Not disgusting, not enjoyable, certainly, the taste was—a sacrifice. It was more like a sound or a color than a taste—but a sound she had never heard, a color she had never seen.

The taste was like a meaning. A belief.

When there was nothing left, she gathered up the fragments of false skin, being careful not to miss any stray wisps, and the clothes he had worn—an ordinary wool suit, shirt, shoes—and put them in the small paper shopping bag she had brought with her. This was important. She would give it to the night manager.

It occurred to her sometimes that they would never let her stop. That was fine. Though at one point she might have dreamed of stopping, she no longer wanted to.

It wasn't even the money, though there was a lot of that.

It occurred to her that she had finally found what it was that she was meant to do, somewhere she could be of use. Here in the night motel, she had found something that quieted the vacant, hopeless pain that seemed to be her most basic state. Had finally found something very much like love. Nuns must feel like this, she decided.

It was good to be needed.

CHAD

KATE RIEDEL

They would eventually call it the Summer of Love, but right then it was only the Spring of Stupidity.

I parked the pickup well off the road and locked it, although there was probably no need. The land Chuck's uncle had lent us for our commune—if I might dignify it with such a name—was in one of the remoter townships of the Georgian Bay area, and no one had lived there for years.

I wiped the sweat from my face and from under my breasts. From now on I was going to wear a bra, in spite of Renata. Renata went smugly bra-less, letting just a suggestion of areola and nipple show through the thin, patchouli-scented, Indian cotton blouses she affected. Okay, so I was jealous. I shouldn't be. Hadn't Chuck told me he liked the earth-mother type?

I wrestled on the backpack, picked up the grocery bags, and started down the trail through the twilit cedars.

I didn't hear him at all. I was forging ahead down the path, head down to balance the weight of the pack, and there in front of me, out of nowhere, was a pair of moccasined feet. Moccasins . . . jeans . . . worn leather belt with a plain brass buckle . . . plaid workshirt . . . raggedly-cut salt and pepper hair just touching the shoulders . . .

He laughed, a deep laugh with five beats to it, and said, "You with that bunch back in the clearing?" The voice matched the laugh, a deep monotone, or rather not a monotone but the seeming lack of stressed syllables that I remembered from my childhood. Tom Crow-Wing had talked like that, stopping to pass the time of day with Dad, back when my Dad was still trying to hack a living out of the bush.

"I didn't hear you," I said, foolishly. His upswept eyebrows disappeared briefly under the ragged edge of his hair. The grey in his hair was deceptive; he was a young man. He laughed that throaty, five-beat laugh again.

"That's my living," he said. He inclined his head toward the bags I'd let drop. "Can I carry those for you?"

Never talk to strangers. My mother told us that, and not just after Dad died and she'd moved us into town. There's plenty of crackpots out in the bush, too. But the bags were damned heavy, and this guy's shoulders were broad.

"Thanks," I said. The trail wasn't wide enough to walk side by side, so I had a good view of those shoulders most of the way back to the clearing.

"What do you do?" I asked, trotting along behind, feeling awkward.

He slowed and turned his head, lifting his flared eyebrows with a half-smile.

"For a living," I added.

"I'm a hunter." He stood aside and let me lead the way into the clearing.

They'd got all the support poles for the longhouse planted in the ground. I'd had my doubts about the book where Chuck had found his plan for building a longhouse, but a longhouse was better than that damned geodesic dome he'd really wanted. Still, I hoped it wouldn't rain; it would be awhile before we had a roof over our heads.

Gavin sprawled beside the fire. Chuck was strumming on his guitar. Renata danced languidly to his aimless chords, her long auburn hair falling silkily over her shoulders. How, I thought despairingly, did she manage to stay looking like that in the middle of the fucking bush? She saw the stranger, stopped, and stared. I did the introductions.

"Renata—Gavin—my boyfriend, Chuck." Too possessive? "I'm Molly."

I stopped and looked at the stranger. He hadn't told me his name, and I hadn't asked. He inclined his head to each in turn, and then gave a name that sounded like little more than vowels to me. But Renata apparently caught it because she held out her hand and said, "Chad? I didn't get the rest of the name?" He didn't answer, so she went on, "It was so sweet of you to help Molly carry things back. Would you like to stay for supper?"

"No, thanks. But I'll bring you supper tomorrow." And Chad, if that really was his name, retreated from the firelight and was gone.

"Oh wow, isn't he handsome?" said Renata. "Do you suppose he's Indian? But I thought they had black eyes. His are such a nice light hazel." She turned to me. "I started supper while you were gone, Molly. I found some potatoes, they were kind of old and icky, but I broke off the sprouts and buried them under the fire. They should be . . . oh, dear," as she raked the blackened lumps out onto the bare ground.

"Renata," I said. "Those were our seed potatoes."

I walked away, leaving someone else to dig the ring bologna and bread out of the grocery bags. That someone else was Renata; her voice carried. "It's not organic—how do we know what's in it?" It didn't matter that much to me anyway; I'd cheated and had a hamburger while I was in Owen Sound.

I spread out my sleeping bag and lay down on top of it. The smell of scorched bologna gave way to the acrid sweetness of marijuana smoke. I drifted off, but woke when Chuck spread his sleeping bag next to mine.

"Renata didn't know those were seed potatoes," he said.

I considered pretending I was asleep.

"She doesn't know as much as you do about these things," he went on. "Try to see Renata's side. She has a really sensitive spirit, you know."

He knew I wasn't asleep, and pretending I was would only make him think I was sulking. "It's all right," I said.

He reached over and pulled me to him, shoving a hand under my jeans and squeezing my rear.

"I'm all sweaty," I said. Meaning, 'You're all sweaty.'

"Mmmm. Sweat turns me on."

So I let him, but my mind wasn't on it.

I'd told Chuck about the bush farm that had finally killed Dad and left Mother bitter. I'd made my childhood sound more glamorous than it was, I suppose; Chuck had the glamour of being a draft-dodger (actually he was 4-F, but he wanted to be a draft-dodger), and I badly wanted him to think me glamorous too. He'd been hurt when I hadn't been enthusiastic about the commune. "You're just jealous of Renata," he'd said. And I was, although I insisted I wasn't. "You know all about living off the land." And that was why I couldn't get enthusiastic about it, but I didn't know how to tell him so. "We need you." I gave in then because I wanted to believe that, and also because I was afraid the next line would be, "All right, I'll go without you."

My mother had not been happy. "I worked so hard to get you and your sister into university, and you throw yourself away on some hippie!" On one level, I couldn't blame her. On another level, she was my mother, she was old, what did she know about youth and love?

Chuck's long curls fell across my face. They were starting to get greasy. Maybe I could rig up a bucket shower, since they had all refused to swim in the river when they found out it had mud and weeds and maybe bloodsuckers. What had they expected, a beach?

Chuck grunted himself to a climax and fell asleep.

Next morning, we found that skunks had been into the groceries. Most of what I'd bought yesterday was a total loss; eggs, bread, bacon, potatoes and onions broken, gnawed, and scattered. The skunks had especially enjoyed Renata's home-made granola. "Didn't you know you should hang them out of reach?" I said.

At least the flour, coffee, and shortening were protected in tins, and we still had some canned stuff. Seeing Renata's face crumple, I softened. "I should have told you about skunks and raccoons. I was just too tired. Never mind, we have some canned beans."

"Beans, beans, good for the heart, the more you eat, the more you fart," Gavin sang. Renata made a face. Chuck didn't say anything, just sat there with that smug look he always put on the morning after to let everyone know he'd had sex.

"I wonder if Chad will be back?" said Renata brightly.

"He's already been," I said. She looked where I was pointing and gave a little squeak.

Two rabbits hung from the longhouse frame, their hind legs looped around the single crosspole in place, the foot of one leg thrust through a slit in the other leg. Tom Crow-Wing had sometimes been carrying rabbits like that when he'd stopped by at our house.

"Oh, the poor things!" said Renata.

Gavin got up for a closer look. "Their throats were cut," he said, sounding as if he wasn't going to be able to keep his beans down long enough to prove the truth of the song.

"They were probably already dead when he cut their throats, that was just to bleed them," I said. I was glad to see they'd also been gutted. "Either of you guys know how to skin rabbits?" I asked, without much hope. They didn't.

I ended up skinning them the best I could with Gavin's new Swiss army knife, the only really sharp knife we had. Dad had liked to have me along on hunting trips, to do the cooking. I'd hoped I'd never have to skin a rabbit again. On the other hand, it was nice to know we'd have something besides bannock and beans for supper tonight.

There were no bullet holes in the rabbits, but then Chad hadn't been carrying a gun. Their necks were broken, so I supposed they'd been trapped, although there were no marks from traps or snares either.

I got the rabbits into the dutch oven and buried the oven in hot coals, while Renata did the dishes and the guys sat around trying to figure out from the book just how to turn a tree into shingles.

"If we're going to have a garden, we'd better get digging," I said to Renata. Renata had been enthusiastic about growing our own vegetables. She was less enthusiastic about attacking the tough sod but I have to hand it to her, she refused to call it quits until I did.

I'd never much enjoyed this kind of work myself. "Let's take a break and look for wild leeks to go with the rabbit," I said finally, and she was happy to drop her spade and follow me through the cedar bush.

Over the crest of the hill, the cedars gave way to mixed hardwood descending to a woody hollow, misty-green with new leaves and carpeted with trilliums. My heart melted with the sudden memory of things that had been good about my childhood on the bush farm; things like this. Then Renata spoiled it all by saying, "Such wonderful, cosmic vibrations—doesn't it make you feel so close to the earth?"

Renata was disillusioned again; leeks didn't just pull out of the ground like green onions, but had to be dug. Somehow, when we were done and trudging back through the cedars, I was the only one with dirty hands and broken fingernails.

"What are these?" asked Renata, stopping and pointing to something at the foot of a tall old cedar.

"Owl pellets." I picked one up to show her the compacted fur and bone, but she made a face so I dropped it.

"We can only make this work if we work together," Renata said as we walked on. "You'll have to learn to share. That's what a commune's all about, you know."

"Huh?" That had come out of the blue.

"Accepting people for who they are, allowing them the freedom to be themselves. You know what I mean."

I didn't, but I could guess.

The guys had managed to cut down a large tree without it falling on either of them.

Renata's enthusiasm for gardening dipped even further during the afternoon. Eventually she wandered off into the cedars. Chuck wandered off into the cedars a little later. I was resting on the spade after digging out a particularly tough section of sod when I felt someone behind me. I turned, and just managed to duck Gavin's mouth on mine.

"I could use a break," he said.

"So could I," I said, maneuvering from between his arms, "but not that kind."

"Aw, come on. What do you think Chuck and Renata are doing right now?"

"If they are, I hope they're doing it in a patch of poison ivy."

"It's people with hang-ups like yours that made the world the mess it is today."

"It's not hang-ups. I'm sweaty, dirty and tired," I said, and went back to digging.

"Uptight bitch," he said, but he left me alone.

Everybody was sweaty and dirty enough by late afternoon to overcome their qualms about swimming in a real river.

We were just finishing supper when Chad turned up. Renata offered him some of the rabbit stew, and Chuck said, "Molly fixed it. Quite the little housewife, Molly is."

"Thank you for the rabbits," I said.

Chad just nodded acknowledgment while he ate, silently and quickly, like the men I remembered from my childhood. As he set the bowl aside he said, in that deep, unaccented voice, "You're right. She'd make a good wife," looking straight across at me.

"Are you an Indian?" Renata piped up.

Chad turned his head toward her without shifting his body.

"Native," he said.

"Far out," said Chuck.

"I'm part Indian," said Renata. "My great-grandmother was a Cherokee princess."

"Really." This time Chad's voice was genuinely expressionless, but I saw a corner of his mouth go up briefly, and I quit being embarrassed for Renata and let myself be amused instead.

Chuck had rolled a joint; he passed it to Renata to light and take the first toke. She passed it to Gavin, who toked and passed it to me. I toked, mostly because Gavin's "uptight bitch" still rankled. I'd never got anything out of it; I faked my highs the way some women fake orgasms. Chad refused, and the joint started the rounds again.

"If you're an Indian, do you know how to build one of those things?"

Gavin asked, gesturing toward the skeleton of the longhouse. Chad turned his head to look. I watched, fascinated. Maybe this was extra-good marijuana; I'd never seen anyone able to turn his head so far without turning his shoulders too.

"No," said Chad, turning back. "I've never needed one."

"Oh." Gavin accepted the joint from Chuck. Chuck felt behind him for his guitar, tuned it, and started to play "Blowin' in the Wind."

I took my toke, handed the joint to Renata, stood up, and started to gather the dirty dishes into the empty dutch oven. "I'll wash them," I said. "No sense putting more temptation in front of the skunks." I headed for the river, followed by "How many years must some people exist / before they're allowed to be free . . ." I scrubbed the dishes, dried them, stacked them back in the dutch oven, and headed back up the trail.

And there was Chad, as if he'd dropped out of the air in front of me, eyes glowing golden in the slivers of moonlight that penetrated the dark cedars. Now what? I thought; another guy who's all hands?

But he didn't touch me, not with his hands. He leaned forward and stroked his right cheek, lightly, against mine. His hair was feather-soft against my face, and as he laughed a low, five-beat laugh I could feel his breath on my ear. Then he moved back, lightly, with another laugh, and said, "I think you would make a good wife."

I could still feel his face against mine, and I couldn't look away from those golden eyes—how could Renata have thought they were hazel?

"You won't have trouble with skunks after tonight," he said. "Would you like me to bring you a chicken tomorrow?"

And then he was gone.

Maybe I really did get high this time, I thought.

I initiated love-making with Chuck that night, I think because I wanted to forget the feel of Chad's hair against my face and his breathy laugh in my ear. It didn't work.

There was a distant scent of skunk in the air the next morning, but our supplies were untouched. Except for the cooking gear; someone had moved the dutch oven to where it would be shaded when the sun rose. I lifted the lid.

"Another present from Hiawatha?" said Gavin, looking over my shoulder.

It was a large chicken, gutted and plucked but not very well plucked, as if it hadn't been scalded first. "We'll have it with dumplings," I said.

Chuck and Gavin set to splitting shingles after breakfast. Renata half-heartedly joined me in breaking more ground. "When do we plant?" she asked.

"If we work hard, maybe this afternoon," I said. That gave her enough incentive we might have done it. Then Gavin yelled, and we turned to see blood pouring out of his leg. I was useless in this kind of emergency and Renata and Chuck weren't much better, but finally we got a t-shirt tied around his leg. Renata drove Gavin into Owen Sound to the hospital.

Chuck helped me finish turning over the garden, and I gave him a hand at splitting shingles, both of us working with commendable caution, and we finished the afternoon with a swim. Despite worry about Gavin, it was a nice afternoon; we were more easy with each other than we had been since we'd first got here.

Renata and Gavin were back in time for supper. Gavin had stitches and a bandage and not much to say. Renata had some flower seeds. I had had too nice an afternoon to point out that replacements for the seed potatoes would have been more useful. She and I even sat down together to plan the layout of the garden.

"Corn, beans and squash," she explained to the guys while I served out the chicken and dumplings. "The Indians called them the three sisters . . ."

Chad stepped into the edge of the firelight. I wondered, as I handed him a bowl, if there was just a faint scent of skunk clinging about him.

"Thanks for the chicken," I said. I avoided looking at him, but I'd never been so acutely aware of anyone's presence before.

Gavin, sitting on a stump to ease the pressure on his injured leg, rolled a joint. It was dark now; the oval moon was well up in the sky. "This is just like when I was a kid at camp," he said. "Anyone know any ghost stories?"

"Maybe there's a ghost in these woods," said Renata. "It's your uncle's land, Chuck. Do you know of any stories?"

Chuck shook his head, expelling his breath. "I wasn't raised around here. How about you, Chad?" He passed the joint to Chad, who shook his head and passed it on to me without toking.

"I know an Algonquin story," he said.

After last night I wasn't sure I wanted to get high; I passed the joint to Renata.

"Is that your tribe?" Renata asked after she'd exhaled. "Algonquin?"

His half-smile came and went, but he didn't answer, only began:

"This is the story of the great horned owl who wanted a wife. He fell in love with a beautiful and accomplished girl, and asked for her hand in marriage. But the girl didn't want to marry an owl, so her parents told the owl no."

I'd heard this story before, from Tom Crow-Wing.

"So the owl took the shape of a handsome young man and came to the girl's village, and the girl, not knowing who he was, agreed to marry him. So they were married."

Chad hesitated, then went on, "And the owl took his new bride by the hand to lead her to his lodge. But on the way, the wind blew his hair back and she saw, instead of ears, the tufts of feathers of the great horned owl. That made her afraid . . ."

That wasn't the way Tom Crow-Wing had told it, but the rest was close: the courtship feast, the story-telling, the ruse of the whispered story to reveal the feathered ears the second time. I only half-listened, taking the opportunity to watch Chad covertly. Renata had been right; he was handsome. His hair might be prematurely grey and hanging any which way, his eyebrows tilted up almost at right angles, and his long nose hooked, as if it had been broken, but it all fit together. And that broad-shouldered body could move so silently, we hadn't known he was there until he stepped into the firelight.

Chad was finishing the story. "Then the owl swooped softly down and took her in his talons and carried her away to his home." He hesitated again, before adding, "And she fell in love with him and they lived happily ever after."

"Like a fairy tale," said Renata.

"Not quite," I said. I stood up and gathered the dirty dishes into the dutch oven. As I started toward the path to the river, I heard Renata ask with a giggle, "What would we find if we looked under your hair, Chad?"

I washed the dishes, stacked them in the dutch oven, and started back through the cedars.

"I hate cedars, they grow so close and dark," my mother had said. And when Chad appeared, silently and suddenly, it was as if the cedars moved in more closely, leaving me no room to sidestep or retreat.

"And what did Renata find?" I asked. "Do you have feathers instead of ears?"

"Why don't you look for yourself?"

"You didn't tell the story right."

"The first part? About how it wasn't the wind but sunrise the morning after the wedding?"

"The last part. That's a fairy-tale ending."

"White people's ending to an Indian story? Why not? You and your friends see nothing wrong with playing at being Indians."

"Not me."

"So why do you play with them? For love?" He moved forward and took the dutch oven from me, and set it down as if he were bowing to me. His arm brushed against mine as he straightened, and we turned, arm brushing arm, back brushing back, until once again we were facing each other, so close our bodies were almost touching. His right cheek caressed mine. His hair, dry, with a clean, slightly dusty scent, fell across my nose and lips as his face moved across mine. I stiffened against the expected hard, open, thrusting kiss, but it didn't come. His mouth was cool, dry and soft, the kiss no more than a feather drawn across my lips, and then our left cheeks were touching, his face rubbing against mine in a gentle up and down motion. His low laugh was like an endearment breathed in my ear.

I looked up. I couldn't see the whites of his eyes, and the rings of gold around his night-widened pupils seemed to glow with a light of their own. I lifted a hand to brush back his hair from his ear, and suddenly his hand was around my wrist, his nails sharp against my skin.

"Not yet," he said, forcing my hand down, not roughly but inexorably. Our faces touched again, he stepped back, released my wrist and was gone.

When I got back to the clearing the fire had died. I was heading toward Chuck's and my sleeping bags when Gavin's voice stopped me. "It's already occupied."

I turned toward the voice. I could see the shadow of Gavin's prone body. Renata's sleeping bag was empty.

"'When I came back to bed, someone had taken my place'," Gavin sang softly. "She said she didn't want to hurt my leg. How about you? Have a little sympathy for the invalid?"

"Get some sleep," I said. "That's what I'm going to do." I snatched up Renata's sleeping bag and lay down on it at the edge of the clearing.

I could hear an owl hooting back in the cedars; the resonant hoo-hoo-oo-hoo-hoo of a great horned owl. If I were to walk quietly back through the cedars, would I see what Tom Crow-Wing had shown my Dad?

"I would have walked right under them if Tom hadn't shown me. Owls. The damnedest thing . . ."

We'd heard him come in. Mother had sent us to bed while she waited up, wrapped in a palpable atmosphere of anger, for Dad to get back. He'd been fishing with Tom Crow-Wing, and there'd been a bottle in his creel. Now his voice, while not slurred, had the careful cadence of making sure the words came out right.

" . . . The damnedest thing," Dad was telling my mother as my sister and I crept down the stairs. "Great horned owls, courting like a couple at a country dance."

Dad dropped the creel on the table. "Like a couple at a country dance, back and forth for hours, swing your partner, like this . . ."

He took my mother's reluctant hand, pulling her up from her chair and toward him, bowing, circling shoulder to shoulder, bodies barely touching in a slow-motion sashay and do-sa-do.

"And then they'd kiss, like this . . ." he rubbed his cheek against hers, gently, up and down. "And he'd tell her he loved her, like this . . ." he put his mouth next to her ear with a quiet, hooting chuckle, "like this . . ." my mother's face softened, and she laughed. Then, over Dad's shoulder, she saw us on the stairs and stopped abruptly, ordering us up to bed. But the atmosphere had softened with my mother's face, and later I heard rare quiet laughter from their bedroom.

"Tell us about the owls," my sister and I had begged Tom Crow-Wing the next day, and he had said, "I'll tell you the story of the great horned owl that we call . . ."

I couldn't remember Tom Crow-Wing's name for the great horned owl, but I remembered how his story had ended. "And she got used to being married to him. Women have to get used to their husbands, no matter who they are." My mother had snorted when she heard that.

"Chicken again?" said Chuck the next morning.

"I don't see you off hunting for the pot," I said. "You're too busy getting a little on the side."

"And what were you doing? It doesn't take that long to do the dishes, and I saw Hiawatha follow you into the woods."

"I didn't think killing chickens qualified as hunting," said Gavin, limping up to take his seat on the stump.

"Children, children," carolled Renata. "We'll never have peace til we learn to share love. Let's shed all these old repressions that made such a mess of the world." Gavin didn't appear to be as convinced of that philosophy as he had been the day before yesterday. Chuck was wearing his smug look.

"Renata's mad at Hiawatha," said Gavin. "He wouldn't let her blow in his ears. He went off chasing you instead. Poor Renata, she wanted to be the first on the block to fuck an Indian."

By the time I'd finished getting the chicken cooking, I'd made up my mind.

"Drive me into Owen Sound, Chuck," I said.

"Why?"

"So I can catch the next bus back to the Toronto, that's why."

"Oh cool off, Molly. What's the big deal? One night with Renata! I'm not laying a heavy on you for whatever you were doing out there in the woods with Hiawatha."

"It's not just that."

"Well, what the fuck is it then?"

"This whole thing. It's not only stupid, it's dangerous. Look what happened to Gavin yesterday. I'm quitting, and the rest of you should, too."

Chuck opened his mouth to protest, then stopped. I turned to see what had caught his eye.

Two men, father and son maybe, stood at the edge of the clearing. They were country people, with the weathered faces, sun-bleached hair and work-worn clothes that distinguished real country people from fake ones like us. Beside me, Chuck gave a little gulp. They stepped forward and I saw they were carrying guns.

"We heard there was some hippies camping out here, but we didn't believe it," said the older one.

"Would you like some coffee?" I said, since no one else seemed ready to speak.

"Don't mind if we do." Chuck sighed in relief as they propped their guns against a tree and came up to the fire. I poured them mugs of coffee and apologized for having no cream or sugar.

"Good coffee, thank you, ma'am," said the older man. The younger one's eyes were glued to Renata's cotton blouse. Renata didn't look ready to shed her repressions with these guys.

"What we're looking for," said the older man, "is there's been an owl after our chickens; got two in the last two days. You seen any sign of owls?"

"We found some owl pellets," said Renata brightly.

"That's true," I said, "but . . ."

Just then a cannonade of caws rose from the cedar woods.

"Never mind!" said the younger man. "Them crows found him for us for sure!" They scrambled up, grabbed their guns and disappeared into the woods, ignoring me when I called after them to stop.

"Why didn't you do something?" I yelled at Chuck. "It's your uncle's land. They're trespassing unless you give them permission."

Chuck looked at me with a funny smile on his face. "It's a good thing you got that chicken into the pot before they turned up," he said. And from behind me Gavin said,

"Hiawatha better hope those guys don't figure out the owl they're really after wears jeans and a flannel shirt."

There were shots in the woods. The crows scattered, the woods fell silent. The men emerged from the trees.

"Missed him," said the younger man in disgust.

"Thanks for the coffee, ma'am," said the older. They disappeared down the trail to the road.

"Just one more day," said Chuck. "Just help Renata put the garden in."

"All right," I said.

Renata faded out when it came time to carry water up to the garden from the river, and the day was nearly over when I headed back from my last water-haul.

As I approached the edge of the clearing, I heard new voices. I set down the bucket and slipped behind a tree. Uniforms. Great; the two men had reported the chicken theft to the Ontario Provincial Police. Chad had brought the chickens, but we'd cooked and eaten them; did that make us accessories? I saw Chuck gesture toward the edge of the trees. This was the time of day Chad always turned up; it looked as if Chuck were trying to cover his ass by ratting on Chad.

We had never seen what direction Chad came from, but if I circled the clearing, maybe I could warn him.

One of the officers was heading for where I stood. The cop was no woodsman; crackling brush gave him away. When I was sure I had lost him, I set out to circle the clearing. The trees here grew too close together for there to be much underbrush, but the crowded younger trees competing with their parents made the going hard even while they lent concealment. I edged between them as quietly as I could, pausing frequently to disentangle my hair and clothes from the clutching branches.

It grew dark, and I was no longer sure of my direction. I turned, hoping to catch a glimpse of our fire, but the trees grew too closely. "I hate cedars," my mother had said. "I feel as if they're crowding in on me, trapping me . . ."

I stood in the dark, forcing myself to relax. As my heart and breathing quieted, I began to hear other sounds; frogs . . . a whippoorwill . . .

A flute. The breathy notes of a small wooden flute playing an unidentifiable but compelling tune.

"Now the owl made himself a magic flute," Tom Crow-Wing had told us, "that played such beautiful music no girl could resist it, and he waited in the woods near the village. He had to wait a long time, because the girl was afraid. But finally the girl decided it was silly to be afraid . . .

I turned slowly to locate the sound. The moon had come out; ahead of me a shaft of silver picked out a clearing. I knew where I was now; where the cedars gave way to mixed hardwoods. Below me the carpet of trilliums glowed silver in the moonlight. Around me, the scent of cedars hung suspended in the remnants of the day's heat.

I followed the music to the last great cedar before the hardwoods. The music stopped. Chad dropped silently to the ground.

"Tell us about the owls," my sister and I had begged. And Tom Crow-Wing had said, "I'll tell you the story of the great horned owl that we call . . ."

Not Chad. The great horned owl, called . . .

"Ke-j'ko-ko-ko'o," I said.

"You say it very well," he said, stepping forward, and leaning toward me repeated his name in my ear, like a throaty chuckle. We began to dance, slowly, forward and back; a slow sashay, always touching, shoulder to shoulder, back to back; and then face to face, close enough to kiss. As our cheeks touched he whispered, "So they were married, and Ke-j'ko-ko-ko'o took her by the hand and led her to his lodge . . ."

Our hands joined. We circled, then came face to face again. His lips moved across mine, across my cheek to kiss my ear.

" . . . where he spread out furs for a bed . . ."

We were so close I could feel the warmth of his body, his heartbeat, through my clothes. I raised my arms to put them around his neck but he stepped back, laughing, circled and leaned forward to lay his face against mine, and said quietly,

"You wouldn't be afraid, would you?"

I shook my head. The movement brought our eyes opposite; great, gold-ringed black pupils staring into mine. His lips met mine in a cool, light kiss and moved across my face to my other ear. "And that night he did for her all that a new husband should do to please a beloved young wife . . ."

His arms were around me like soft, quiet wings. I raised my hands to his thick, feathery hair and whispered "Ke-j'ko-ko-ko'o," a name like rare laughter.

I got back to the clearing next morning to find everything packed into the pickup.

"Where were you?" Chuck said. I didn't bother to answer, only asked,

"What's going on?"

Chuck didn't answer, so Gavin did.

"Fearless leader here," he said, "doesn't know how to read maps."

I looked at Chuck. He just picked up his guitar and headed down the path. Gavin snickered.

"This isn't his uncle's land. His uncle's land is half a mile downriver. The OPP were here last night to kick us off."

"It was very nice of the owner," said Renata, "not to press charges."

The house I live in now is on the edge of town, just across the road from woods and open country. The wood is a protected area, and a good thing, too, because some of the neighbors don't like owls. They say owls kill cats. Even the neighbors without cats complain that the mating calls, early in the year, keep them awake.

I don't mind. Women get used to their husbands, no matter who they are.

TAKE THE 'A' TRAIN

WAYNE ALLEN SALLEE

Cassady spent October in his dingy, three-room hovel, submerged in his own guilt, self-exiled from the city. He ventured out rarely, and then only for food. His phone was disconnected on the twentieth, three days after the girl's murder. ComEd hadn't taken care of the lights yet, so he was able to spend the days watching television, safe from the prying eyes of the neighborhood. He watched situation comedies from the 1960s, mostly shows with father figures.

The scar on his hand was healing nicely. And on Halloween, Cassady stayed in the corner tavern for three beers and nobody had asked him any questions. That made him feel better, feel as if he could tackle the world again.

When he went home from the bar, Cassady spent long, quiet moments contemplating the Terri Welles centerfold on his bedroom wall. He decided he would talk to Sarah about the murder the next afternoon.

The first of November came in with a freezing downpour, but the rain did not deter Cassady from waiting the half-hour for the train to Sarah's flat on the north side. The four-car El was delayed by what the conductor said was a police- and gang-related incident, and when it finally did arrive, icicles were forming in Cassady's beard. He cursed an elderly woman for not boarding the train faster. She had begun to say something in return, but stopped when she saw the hatred in his eyes.

He stood commando-style against the sliding, graffiti-washed doors. Let someone try and make him move out of the way! He scanned the faces of the others in his car carefully, but did not see the killer's face or anybody else's that was recognizable. This was a city of strangers. He would leave soon, yes oh yes. No one knew him anymore. He would go to Boston or . . . New York City. It was a grim resolution.

The train wormed underground, avoiding the rich bankers and pretty secretaries who lived and/or worked on Rush Street and the Gold Coast. Cassady knew in his mind that it was not always this way; the fatcats and moneymakers had forced the city government to change the tracks to fit their needs. But Cassady didn't think the train was an eyesore. The pretty stewardesses and waitresses who lived on Sandburg Terrace could fuck themselves. He was glad that the Tylenol Killer had been able to kill at least one of them. Whoever he had been, if Cassady had known him, he would have told the killer to put cyanide in all the bottles in the Walgreen's on Rush Street. Then they all would have died. Forty minutes later, Cassady stepped off the train at Addison. He was humming Van Morrison's "Brown-Eyed Girl."

Picking up a copy of the *Tribune*'s Green Streak at a corner kiosk on Waveland that smelled like crap, Cassady read that a suspect had been questioned as the El Murderer. Cassady was shocked to find out that Quita McLean's knife-killing was the third in the last four weeks. Why hadn't he read about the others? Were the papers covering this up like they did everything else? Were there people out there who maybe had witnessed one of the other murders like he had? Maybe seen the killer's face? Would they be sympathetic towards him or hate him?

Cassady pressed his fists to his forehead, dropping the paper. Two Hispanics in leather blazers stared at him from across the street.

Witnesses . . . the thought made him shiver. He was getting sick again, just like Martin Balsam in *The Taking of Pelham One, Two, Three*. The city was killing him. Sarah would help ease his suffering, though, like she always had.

Wait. Someone was watching him from behind.

Turning quickly, Cassady saw no one. Perhaps the watcher was some kind of acrobat and was now hiding behind the newspaper stand? Turning back, he saw the blond man staring, white hairs sticking out of his beard like weeds. Red veins quavered in his eyes. Cassady suddenly realized that he was staring into mirrored glass.

He walked towards Broadway in the quickening darkness, leaves piled like ashes all around him. Cassady had known Sarah since his freshman year at the University of Illinois on Polk Street. 1980. Geez, six years that seemed like yesterday. He still couldn't find a decent job.

Sarah had tawny hair and almond brown doe eyes. Cassady felt himself getting an erection. Once, when he was awakened after dozing on the bus and dreaming of Sigourney Weaver, Cassady was embarrassed to discover that he was the proud owner of a raging hard-on and at least three bus passengers were aware of it. They had tittered amongst themselves, thinking everything was funny as usual. If only more people could be concerned with what was happening in the real world. After the bus incident, Cassady learned to sleep with a copy of the *Trib* over his lap, even if he was only daydreaming.

Sarah had taken up nursing after graduation. He had dropped out in his junior year at the U of I. She still loved him, though. The suspected killer's name was David Spellman, age 27, unemployed. Chicago's Finest had found him in an alleyway behind Winchell's Donut House. He was in the process of raping a fifteen-year-old girl. He had a broken Coke bottle in one hand, and still had not actually confessed to anything. Cassady reeled off the stats from the newspaper article as if he had been reading the back of a Topps baseball card. He did not realize he was talking out loud.

He knew them all, though. Manson. Speck. Son of Sam. And Gacy, just five Christmases ago. What was that joke . . . Gacy's favorite country and western song: "I'm walking the floor over youuu . . ." His voice trailed in mock falsetto, echoing madly in the shadowed corners of New Town. Some people thought the gays deserved it, deserved getting picked up by

Gacy and shown the old handcuff trick. Cassady didn't think so, though. Gays were different, but that was no reason to kill them.

The paper also had a short piece about the man who had found Quita McLean's body. It was on page three of the Chicagoland section, next to an ad for Field Days.

Sarah Dunleavy lived in a second-floor walkup at 1123 Wolfram. Wrigley Field was a short distance away, and as he trudged towards Sarah's block, Cassady imagined opening day of the '86 season. Maybe this would be the year the Cubs would take it. He remembered all the times his mother had taken him to the weekend games with the Cardinals and Mets. The smell of hot dogs and pizza, watching couples hold hands, yelling when Banks or Santo hit one out on Sheffield. Songs on the radio . . .

(Do you remember when, we used to sing, shala la la?)

Well, shala la la, here he was. He scratched nervously at his right hand before ringing the bell.

(Whatever happened to Tuesday and So Slow?)

He wondered whatever happened to Van Morrison, the Dave Clark Five, Paul Revere & The Raiders.

"Denny!" Sarah said buoyantly in the open doorway. She was wearing Levi's and a loose-fitting burnt-orange sweater. The sleeves were pushed up around her elbows. When they kissed, Cassady felt that she still wasn't wearing a bra. "Bet you're hunger after that long train ride, huh?"

"Yeah." Cassady tried not to sound distracted. "You bet."

He sat at the kitchen table while Sarah busied herself with the dinner. She turned now and then to ask a question, her hair falling across her face. He was happy that she was not wearing make-up or nail polish. That was for the sluts who worked downtown.

He made small talk about the weather and his job interviews and then stared at the flowered wallpaper until Sarah walked to his seat with the prepared meal.

(Countin' flowers on the wall, that don't bother me at all)

They walked together into the living room and sat near the television. Sarah placed a steaming plate of roast beef and mashed potatoes on the tray next to him. She poured a Pepsi into his glass. He watched it fizz, as if it was something mystical.

"Hey, thanks," Cassady said, smoothing his shirt.

Sarah sat back on the sofa and watched him eat. Using the remote, she turned on the television. He was grateful when Sarah switched from the news to a rerun of "Barney Miller."

Cassady slowly cut into the meat. It was rare, his favorite. The knife scraped against the ceramic plate, and the juice sprayed finely onto the sleeve:

(The juice erupted from the woman's breast and soaked his sweater)

he watched it spread into the cotton blend like a hideous sunset, and he pushed his plate away in disgust;

(because she was dead and his hand o god his hand held the bloody knife)

and Sarah looked away from one of Dietrich's witticisms to Inspector Luger at the sudden jangling of the plate.

"This steak is too damn rare," Cassady spat, needing something to say.

"Denny," Sarah exclaimed, wiping her hands down the sides of her jeans. "You always order it that way everywhere we go. You know how the waitresses all think you're some kind of a werewolf!"

"The waitresses don't know shit!" Cassady hissed.

"Denny, what the *hell* is the matter with you?" Concerned lines found their proper place on Sarah's face.

Cassady's hands played twister with his hair. His eyes were squeezed shut. Minutes passed thickly.

Finally, with Cassady staring at the powder-blue carpet, and Sarah looking at him, studying him the entire time, he spoke. He explained that he was having a rough time finding a job since his unemployment ran out, and that his shoulder was sore again because of the damp weather. Sarah understood him well. And oh how she loved him. Soon, they were laughing about the new Woody Allen film, and about snoopy old Mrs.

Spinoza next door. They talked about dinner on the lakefront that summer, Christmas shopping, and the taverns on Division Street. Then Cassady's face clouded over as fast as a schizoid's, as if he had just remembered why he had come.

"You know, Sarah," he said softly. She stopped smiling. "Well, I sort of knew this girl once. She worked down the mall from me when I was at the jeans place. A few of the girls at the store used to go to lunch with her."

Cassady was speaking in a detached way, strangely formal, as one might speak to an old friend at a wake. Sarah studied his face more closely, looking for some clue as to his behavior.

"It's been almost two years since the night she didn't come home," he continued. "She was a lot like me, you know. She really loved the city. Not being afraid to go out at night like just about everybody else."

"I'm not afraid," Sarah interrupted softly.

"I know." Cassady didn't hear what she said. "I guess that's why I still think about her

(sometimes I'm overcome thinking about it, making love in the green grass)

even though I only met her once or twice. She reminded me so much of myself. I don't know . . . it's hard, Sarah. It's hard to explain why I love it here so much. Yeah, I know. You can't walk around smiling without people thinking you're gay or retarded or something.

"But, let me tell you something, Sarah

(behind the stadium with you)

on a day when everybody and every*thing* spits in my face, I love it here that much more.

(my brown-eyed girl)

"It was December. This one girl I knew, Karen—she was manager of my store at the time—she told me how her and Vicki used to sit in the front of Foxmoor's, and that's what they had done that last day, eating lunch on the floor because it was so crowded with Christmas shoppers, and they were throwing fries at each other, making faces at the shoppers. And that night, Vicki went to a bar and never came home.

"This wasn't a bar in a rough neighborhood or something," Cassady said, shaking his head. "It was in Palos Heights, for chrissakes, four blocks from her home."

More silence. A car honked outside. A door upstairs slammed distantly.

"They found her in January. This farmer up near the Wisconsin border let his dog out one morning, and . . . this is how the paper put it: 'After several minutes of digging in the snow, the dog ran proudly back to its master, the head of the missing girl jauntily dangling from his mouth.' Jauntily dangling. Jesus, can you believe that? The coroner put the time of death at about a week before that. There were pieces of her all over the field."

His hands were still pressed tightly against his skull. Cassady made claws out of his fingers and dug them into the creases around his forehead, as if trying to re-open a line of sutures that held back a slow trickle of mistakenly discarded memories. He thought of the blood dripping down Quita McLean's thigh, black in the glow of the streetlamps. Just like the others. He did not mention that he had asked Vicki out to dinner, and that she had refused, placing him in the class of all the other macho animals. Sarah didn't need to know that.

Sarah had begun to speak when Cassady lifted his head. The blood vessels stood out in his cheeks from where his palms had pushed against the skin. Several thin red scratches ran across his forehead. My God, Denny used to have laugh lines, Sarah thought.

The clock behind Cassady read ten o'clock. Over two hours had passed. A rerun of "M*A*S*H" was on the television.

"No," Cassady said with a tone of finality, knowing what Sarah was going to ask. Oh he knew her only too well. Women were all alike, really. "They thought it was her boyfriend, but they couldn't be sure."

He stopped talking then. He was thinking about other, more private things. Sarah reached across the distance between them and took his hand, wiping the blood that was on his nails, soothing him just like she did in that dream thousands of years before. Yes, she knew him well. Too well.

Cassady knew this, knew that it was only a matter of time before the cops came and asked her questions. He really had only one choice.

Sarah slowly realized the change that was occurring in Cassady. He looked too calm. Too serene. Instead of wondering why he had brought up all these memories, tragic as they were, she felt chilled.

Denny's eyes were different, she thought.

"Denny, I—"

"Sarah, wait. Do you remember a few years ago, it was round the time of the Humboldt Park riots, that girl who was raped near the Belmont El?

"Remember that guy, he was a clerk in a record store, and he tried to help, and the guy stabbed him to death?"

"Denny, you can't blame yourself for what happened to that girl at work," Sarah said. "You weren't even with her the night it happened, you couldn't possibly have saved her."

She shivered in the semi-darkness of the room.

"You're right about the city, though. You can only pray it doesn't happen to you.

"Now, c'mere."

She pulled him towards her, burying his face into her blond hair.

"You know," Cassady spoke into Sarah's breasts. "I'm not like the others . . . like that old bag Spinoza next door. I'm not afraid of the streets."

"Nobody said you were, Denny," Sarah said, slowly rocking him back and forth in her arms. "C'mon. I'll make you a drink."

She stood up, ruffling Cassady's hair as if he were a child's plaything, and walked across the room to the small bar that stood against the wall. There were only two bottles on the shelf: a full bottle of Seagram's and a half-empty fifth of DuBouchett's Blackberry Brandy, for when Sarah's father came by to see how his little girl was doing on her own.

"I'm . . . not sure why you told me these things, Denny," Sarah repeated. "But, don't blame yourself. Believe me."

"You're right." Cassady's voice was like a metronome. "Life's too short."

He covered his eyes with his hands again. Without stopping, he told

Sarah about the October night on the El platform, about being a spectator to death. In his head he was singing

(making love in a rock bed)

Sarah spilled much of the bottle's contents on the counter.

(beneath the subway tracks with you)

Cassady slowly took his hands from his face. Without stopping, he let the knife drop into Sarah Dunleavy's back. Much of her blood spilled onto the counter.

(my brown-eyed girl)

The next several hours were a nightmarish blur. Conspiracy blended with paranoia, enveloping Cassady the moment he left Sarah's apartment. His face was no longer familiar. He was wearing the same type of mask that all the other faces were wearing. Every day of their stinking lives. The cops wouldn't even question his motive. They would nod their heads in agreement and maybe even buy him a beer after he told them the reason he killed the love of his life SarahSarahSarahhhh.

He grabbed a too-inquisitive squirrel and squeezed its steaming guts onto the dying grass as if the rodent were toothpaste. Squirrel-honey, your gums are bleeding because of gingivitis, you dumbshit. Better use Colgate. Ha! He named the squirrel Binky. R.I.P., Binky, old buddy. Hasti Spumanti.

It was a Bad Day at Black Rock, all right. First Sarah and her incessant whining over his looks and that stupid laugh that sounded like a freaking air hose! And the rain was making the dead space in his right bicep throb as if the muscle was still there. Fucking doctors, eight years ago said it'd be all right. Yeah, all the interns at the Osteopathic Hospital were aware of his case, nodding their heads in agreement, saying the muscle would be back in the next six months. Liars! Didn't they realize muscles are what girls wanted? They were too busy making their six-figure incomes anyway . . .

Cassady bought a pint of Seagram's, downed it while crossing a public park, and threw the empty bottle with all his might. He clapped in glee when the bottle smashed against the wall of a recreation center, shattering the gang graffiti and lovers' initials.

He ran screaming down a deserted midnight street. No one looked out their windows, and, knowing this, Cassady smiled broadly and winked at the clouds above.

He shared secrets with the drainage ditches.

Somehow finding his way uptown to Sheridan, Cassady raced madly for the El tracks intersecting the street at Loyola. He fell down, chipping a front tooth. Swinging a ragged fist, he mouthed bloody epithets at several singing winos behind the ruins of the Grenada theater.

He had to get to his train. Pull a train. The train of thought. He had lost his train of thought. Hey, where did we go, days when the rain came? All along the waterfall with you, my brown-eyed girl. On Slate Street that grate street I saw a man he dry humped his wife, a Chicano made moan sound Ha! I saw a man he danced with a knife in Chicago oh please come to Boston in the springtime . . . the train! It was coming, he could make it

(underneath the subway tracks with you)

(my brown-eyed girl)

the train. A giant, throbbing penis that screwed Cassady every time he took its sterile ride for a job interview. Or for a pick up.

The turnstile of the Loyola station wavered in front of him, a gateway to truth, an upright skeleton of a dead centipede. Glazed with ice, it blazed like neon blue in Cassady's brain.

He found the needed energy to run towards it, making the distance easily in seven long strides. But the bars moved clockwise, providing an exit for the commuters inside. It was not intended to be an entrance. The bars did not budge and Cassady was beyond hearing his nose crack. His lips curled in a snarl and his teeth touched the frozen metal.

He stepped back, lunged forward three more times, each time harder than the previous, stopping only when a triangular swatch of his cheek was ripped from his face. A bone shard, fingernail-thin and red in the night, peeked through Cassady's right eyelid like a sentry. Scouting a new way to get into the fortress.

He left the turnstile, then. Stumbling towards the closed glass doors. Flecks of his face trailed behind.

The door was locked. He did not hesitate, and by crashing through it, gouged his already blinded eye. When he hit the ground, something broke deep inside him, making a pulpy sound, perhaps that of crushing grapes for wine.

His legs made mock parodies of each other as he fell forward along the concrete floor. Muttering incoherent thank yous that it was too late for a teller to be on duty, Cassady crawled up the iced stairs, ten twenty thirty leading upwards into a mist. Darkness clutched at his one remaining eyelid.

When he heard the quiet rumble of the approaching train, not realizing that the Loyola terminal was closed for repairs, he finally relaxed.

He cried as the train went by, a thunderous blur of winos and late-night partyers, none so much as noticing his outstretched, supplicating arms.

He cried louder, in great sobs spewed from his throat like vomit. Then he saw the man, so much like him, dragging his body away from Cassady as if Cassady himself was some kind of psycho pariah. Or was that messiah?

The similar man undid the buttons on his shirt in painful slowness. Would anybody care if Cassady did kill himself, like he knew the other man was going to do? He was sure his parents didn't even know he was living in Chicago. The last time he had written them, years before, he had told them he was working for the government. Would his face be in the paper? Pull a train, pull the cord tighter tighter honey honey sugar sugar yummy yummy. My brown-eyed girl.

Tying the knot was easier than he had expected, even with the skin peeling off his fingers in the pre-dawn cold.

The other man, now nothing more than a shadow, climbed on top of the salt box next to the stairwell. He waited for Cassady to decide. So, it was going to be a game of chicken! Cassady would show them all!

The other man, now just a mist, painstakingly tied one shirt sleeve around his tired neck.

And on a blustery night in early November, long after the Night Owl train was lost in the distance of the skyline, Dennis Cassady watched with numb fascination as the crazy man hung himself with the remains of his blood spattered shirt. He was afraid to make a move.

Of course, there were no living witnesses.

C2

ANKE KRISKE

In my living room lies a body battered bloody. She's my neighbor, a busybody. I don't remember her coming inside my little apartment. C2. That's my number. C for Ceilia, 2 for . . . second incarnation? Certainly I'm not what I once was. Neither is Mrs. Hernandez. I suppose it's possible that she came in uninvited while I was taking a shower, tripped and hit her head on my only end table; but there really is too much blood for that. It looks more like someone had taken the heavy coffee pot and bashed in her face.

Assuming there is a body.

I sit down crosslegged on the floor—uncarpeted, cold at this time of the morning—and observe. She's wearing a faded flowered housecoat. Her hair is in curlers. There's blood on Mrs. Hernandez's face, what I can see of it, since she is lying rigidly face down. One of her moccasin slippers has fallen off. Her toenails are painted bright red. Funny, because she doesn't wear nail polish on her fingers and never uses make-up.

Just this once she may be solid and dead, and I will have to call the police and they will finally take me away and lock me up in some brick institution surrounded by sweeping green lawns. I do hope she dissolves.

I've had hallucinations before. I accept with equanimity the appearance of a possibly dead woman lying in my living room. I do not believe I am dreaming: other events appear in normal order and cover a natural span of time. I could touch her. My hallucinations are mostly visual, occasionally audible, but never tactile.

And yet I won't reach out. I would really be displeased to find that she is real. Her blood would stain the floor, and I would lose my damage deposit when they come to take me away.

So I get up and pace to the grimy window and back to the corpse. I should feel more concern for a human being who has suffered and died prematurely. A flattening of emotions is not a good symptom, I have been told.

Assuming I have a dead body lying at my feet.

What if I don't? Then I am equally mad, though perhaps not a menace to others. This isn't, after all, a fleeting hallucination. Would I feel indifferent if I were crossing the street and a car careened toward me? Could I be mugged and simply stare at my assailant? My mind still functions more or less in the approved manner, but normal emotions are lost to me.

I drop my face into my hands. If I could just summon up the fear of madness to dissolve my hallucination or the courage to confirm reality by calling on a neighbor for assistance. The body lies there. I can only stare and wait and hope. I don't want to be lost to the dark places. Psychiatry is voodoo, a faith in magical powders and words and a denial of failure.

"Ceilia, what are you doing?"

A face in the door. That face should be on the corpse, though she wears jeans and her hair is combed out. I blink. Now which is reality and which is illusion? "Yes?"

"You didn't answer when I knocked."

Failure to respond to stimuli. "I didn't hear you."

"I just came to tell you that I'm fine. It was just a little nose bleed. You looked as if you were ready to pass out."

"I've never been very good at the sight of blood, Mrs. Hernandez." Oh, yes, we had bumped into each other in the hallway.

She steps onto her corpse. "Are you feeling all right?" That is not what she wants to ask. She sees the madness in me.

"I didn't sleep well." That is all I can manage. And I am hardly aware that she closes the door, leaving me alone with her dead shell.

THE ROSEGARDEN

SETH MATTHEW LINDBERG

Once the city has you, you can never get out alive. But maybe for a night you can dance, preen, and linger at a club and lift your spirits above the maze of streets on wings made of music. Jack knew that, threading his long legs every Monday night for the Rosegarden, each week a different club or warehouse or drafty basement of a bar.

They kept the location secret to keep out Ren Fair losers with their long hair and flowy shirts, the gawkers and the smug-looking computer industry boys quaffing their microbrews and scanning the area, taking in each detail to relate to their less adventurous co-workers and their distant Internet-lovers-of-the-week.

Jack didn't know any of the people at the Rosegarden. Every week like another: down some stairs following a length of string through a back alleyway, stepping over a homeless vet sleeping in a pool of his own urine mixed with vomit, cradling his bottle like Linus with a security blanket. Knock on which door? The left one . . . no answer, the right. And down a hallway, ducking the hanging bare bulbs and the network of pipes over his head.

The people at the door, always the same people, took whatever Jack would give them. Sometimes three bucks and laundry quarters, sometimes a ten dollar bill, sometimes the last of his change, ignoring pleas either way for his money back or to let him in just this once, shepherding him through the door or archway or hung black tarp and onto the mist-covered floor.

But always, always, he brought a rose: the true price of admission. Each rose was added to the bundle of others by the door before they led him in. Were he older or younger, he would have scoffed at the pretentiousness of it all. In that year, however, he always managed to find a rose and never thought the least of it.

Even among the long, thin creatures in impeccable fashions, he never felt out of place. He never wondered why he always managed to find the club. He perched himself where he could be ignored yet take in the most of the scene: he never bothered to stop and reflect how out of place he always looked.

He often dreamed of walking over and talking to one of the many women who frequented the club. At times he felt their eyes upon him and wondered if they were inviting him to introduce himself. He'd toy with a strand of his bleached-out mohawk, down because he was lazy, and pulled back into a loose pony-tail. He'd rub his face, pull up the collar of his battered trench coat, and wonder if they appreciated the band on his tee shirt.

There was the longhaired Asian girl, her mouth lipstick-painted into a perpetual downward bow. Her thin features tilted into a slender body, the collar always up on her sleeveless velvet dress. The girl who wore the raven's wings that first night Jack came to the club. Tall, green-eye, not attractive as much as *striking* in some bottom-of-the-spine sort of way.

Two tiny girls who looked like twins perched like carrion birds. They kept their heads shaved and wore New Wave makeup to augment their minidresses that looked for all purposes to be made out of trash-bags or, depending on the week, plastic wrap.

The girl with the daring smile, flashing black doll-like eyes, the one who always wore gloves. She toyed in a flirtatious dance with an extremely tall gentleman who preferred velvet tights and tailcoats and danced in a manner awkward and graceful, sacred and profane.

Jack never saw the kind of girls he liked here, but that's not why he came night after night. Oh, sure, the first few weeks he had his hopes up, but soon he fell into a rhythm. The rhythm meant he had to observe, and occasionally dance, but never interfere, never interact. He kept this unspoken rule, frightened of crossing the line and never being invited back again, never knowing where to go. Never being able to smile mysteriously or bandy out the name of the *Rosegarden* to his stupid high school gamer friends who'd heard of the name somewhere but didn't, and probably never would, quite understand the significance.

The rule meant he wouldn't go too far, never touch the surface or disrupt the skein of isolation that had been so precariously set up: like putting your fingertips through water, watching the ripples go out and away in bands.

Of course, you came for attraction, but you stayed for the music, you stayed for the spectacle, you stayed for the *dance*. Jack never heard the music he heard at other clubs, and as the music scene started changing, he never saw the Rosegarden's playlist vary. Not once, not even the moment's thought of a techno or top forty or swing or anything. Rarely, even, he heard the bands he wore on his tee shirts in his hopeless attempt to impress. The songs kept from one beat to the next, a thudding chorus of pops and scratches and bass lines, and rising above it were the peaks and desolate lows of the melody. He heard traces of modern instrumentation, distortion mixed with the harpsichord, violin, cello. The music rising, again, higher, higher, then falling away from the structure like leaves in autumn.

Chaos: and the dancers wilt, or stand there, or run off the floor, or palsy like marionettes with tangled strings. Then through the trickle of fading crashes, and bass line rises up again, throbbing like a heartbeat, and one by one the dancers move as if the strings that held them take life, one by one.

And, sometimes, the sound of a woman's voice, far away. The voice seemed to whisper: *We will use these things to fly far away . . .*

There were nights when Jack went to find that he was the only one not in costume. Once, the entire club and each visitor dressed themselves as if they were Venetians in white, with porcelain masks adorning their faces and brocaded in authentic clothing, coats, corsets, and stockings all in ivory.

Another night simulated Poe's Masque of the Red Death, in a particular winding upstairs warehouse of long rooms, from one color to the next (and rarely did the trussed inhabitants stray from room to room). Jack didn't enter the Red Room, nor talk to the sole inhabitant, though he had half a mind to. That was his night to try to make conversation. He failed, each time.

For a week he fashioned a pair of wings to match one of the girls, but found he couldn't make them the way he wanted to. He stretched the wings and nailed them to his wall. Their imperfections mocked him every night.

Then one night he spotted another like him, among the angular dancers, the black feathers, and the dry-ice fog. A short, boxy girl in an ill-fitting antique dress. She wore her hair back over one ear with a barrette and looked like she chewed on fingernails half-lacquered with nail polish.

Jack immediately became infatuated with her.

He went to approach her, but she spied his presence and darted away towards a door that from its crude marks he guessed was a restroom. He sighed and waited for her at the bar, but she never returned, another ghost in this menagerie of the Rosegarden.

But the music remained, hypnotic, speaking of the tribal and the industrial, the spare and the arcane. It never changed at the Rosegarden, not like Jack wanted it to. And the deejays never took requests.

Something in Jack, however, changed the night he saw normalcy in his dreamlike dance. It tugged at his spine, it caressed his insides, though he couldn't name it or put a face to his feelings. The appearance of this girl put a flaw in this brilliant gem of his Monday nights.

He never for once thought of how *he* must look, coming each night, in his tattered trench and hastily tied-up hair.

All through the weekend he'd stress out, waiting for the slip of paper under the door of his room in the flat he rented out with friends he no longer talked to. Or the message on his phone. He spent his time instead of waiting for the sign, to seek it out, by scouring the bathrooms of the coffeehouses near where he or his friends lived. He walked along the busy streets inspecting every telephone pole for hidden signs within the bland and vapid pronouncements of this band or that club, this new style or fashion or movie or anything that the *others* ate, the *others* consumed. The Others.

Preparing, those Monday nights, meant scouring through the wardrobes of his friends or pasting together things found on the street. Procuring, and usually succeeding, in the chemicals he needed. Alcohol would do in a pinch: it was a depressive, yes, but it did lower inhibitions. But stimulants worked best. Keep high, and edgy, and with that hungry look. Any drug would do if it meant he looked like he didn't give a fuck.

The night after he saw the girl he spent the majority of the evening clutching his stomach from the gut-wrenching bathtub crank he'd bought from some bikers who were friends of friends. He'd kept his face a mask of tooth-grinding perma-joy mixed with the utter agony of whatever they'd mixed it with that caused his stomach to convulse. The concentration helped him to spike his hair up in a mohawk that looked like fishhooks made of hair in rows down the back of his head.

He'd wrapped black duct tape (it *hurt*) around his frail chest and poured himself into borrowed PVC pants. He painted himself with war paint like he'd seen in the Anthropology texts he'd half read while in his first and only year of college. He found two roses, and spray painted one black.

It took longer than usual to hunt for the club, scaring a group of junkies half to death on the way asking for directions. By the time he'd made it to the club, the crank had hit and gone and left him shaking and bad in every way, his molars near ground to powder and he in one of those introspective-as-fuck moods.

He'd shown up with two roses, but the person at the door would only take one. He tried to make her choose, but she refused, and only with nervous looks between her and the bouncer was Jack galvanized into placing the solitary white rose in with the rest. He also gave the door-keepers a photocopied slip of paper. They took it with impassively bewildered faces.

The note read: "Have you seen her?"

He stalked through the club, past the leggy dancers and slender, willowy figures in the gloom. The club was that night in the back of a warehouse out by the waterfront, surrounded on all sides by the walls of the warehouse, with empty sky and that yellowed orb of a moon rising above.

The motif of this night was apparently trees. All of the figures were dressed in bodystockings and wrapped with shiny black material, which fell off their bodies like leaves. Their fingers and often arms were extended out to resemble limbs and branches, and throughout the club elaborate headdresses was the motif.

Jack, in his white war-paint speckled in blue, out of place and yet within it all at the same time, standing out and being part of the mesh. He stood angrily thinking near a few buckets of dry ice that kept the area in waist-high mist.

Why am I annoyed at her? he wondered. He honestly didn't know. But yet, her presence the other night infuriated him. He frowned, and pulled out a cigarette to smoke, his brow furrowing and greasepaint collecting in the wrinkles.

He fell into a depression, the only solace that he had at least understood his anxiety. And only the rising movements of the music brought him out of his black mood, only the odd, creaking dances of the assembled masquers as they lifted their branchlike arms to the sky caused him to forget his overanalyzing mood.

The boxy girl in the dream did not show, at least, not that Jack saw.

Jack's life got worse, like a treadmill. He walked down the same endless city streets to one job or another. His ancestors had created the city, raising up the streets and watching the buildings rise, only to be trapped within. To die slow, alcoholic deaths. To meet their maker with their heads turned over one shoulder, frightened of imaginary pursuers.

He worked retail and warehouse jobs to keep the creditors at bay, to keep one step ahead of them. He worked his fingers to the bone maintaining the city, dreaming only of the Rosegarden.

Sometimes he dreamed of being chased through the empty streets by a gigantic man with a bull's head and three-piece suit, only to wake to hear the phone ring and listen to how concerned a credit card company was about his fiscal health.

Months later, Jack thought he saw her on the street. At night, when he was leaving his flat and walking down the street towards the more familiar thoroughfares. He shouted after her, but she ignored him, turned a corner and disappeared.

He thought about her constantly. Yet, he couldn't truly remember her face.

The night he wore gray, painted his body silver, and slicked back his hair, he saw her again. He couldn't be sure: through the mirrorshades he wore, most appeared as shadows in the darkness and flashing lights, but there was a determination and normalcy to her gait that the others lacked. The silent, fey-like beasts stepped and pranced past her wearing animal masks and Victorian corsetry, female and male dancers, and there was a face in a simple mask and a determined stride.

By that time of the night, the floor was littered with the tiny handbills he'd passed out to everyone, asking plainly, "Have you seen her?" They looked like white specks amongst the movements of the shadows behind his sunglasses. He sort of liked the effect.

He slipped through the crowd towards the figure, emulating the shadows' graceful yet alien movement. He forced himself to think of nothing while approaching her.

I only have this one chance.

He twisted, slipping past two languid dancers to stretch his arm out.

His long fingers grasped her soft shoulder. He immediately felt the worn fabric of her dress, soft and yet harsh against his fingertips, the giving texture of her flesh.

She turned, and even through his mirrorshades, he saw her look of fear and surprise. As a long man with the mask of a cat slipped past, his whiskers eerily twitching, she looked back at Jack, her surprised expression fading to one of pain. "Let me go," she said over the music.

"I've been looking for you," he responded.

"I know . . ."

He felt possessed with urgency. "What's your name?"

"You shouldn't do this?"

"What's your *name?*" he asked again, and clutched her shoulder tighter.

"Ganit," she blurted. "You shouldn't do this?" she repeated, urgently.

"I'm Jack," he said. She just looked at him.

A woman with an elaborate mask of an antelope passed by, turning her head their way. She was cinched into a tight, whalebone corset, and walked in tiny steps. Jack glanced at her, then back at Ganit's steady eyes.

Jack let go, and the girl turned and walked off.

He felt a vague tug at the bottom of his stomach, possessed by a sudden fear he had no words to describe.

The rest of the night he felt it, aware of her watching him from places he couldn't see. His night was ruined by the thought of her watching him.

She knows I'm here, he thought. *Things can never be the same.*

He pushed his sunglasses back up, watching the shadows through his shades. *But I must find a way . . . to go back to that time. When I didn't care, when this was all some dream. Something special that I visited.*

When the girl with the raven's wings walked by, he did the unspeakable and reached out to grab her. Rudely, he mashed his body against hers.

He felt her cold body, hard yet strangely pliant. As he looked behind her face contorted with fear and into those expressionless eyes, he suddenly knew what he had to do.

Dropping her suddenly, so that one wing folded over in a

painful-looking way, he ducked out of the Rosegarden and into the chilly midnight air.

The next week he didn't go, though it tortured him not to. He found the invitation anyway, a curious overphotocopied picture of a rose, the grayscale turning into twisted zebra-striped lines. A tiny address for a warehouse in the southern part of the city. He let it go like he'd let his phone bill and credit cards go. Like the horrible job he'd forced himself to go to every night for a year to pay the minimums on bills that would never go away. So he could listen to his coworkers blather about babies and television and every useless and stupid thing this world has created, so he could work to exhaustion pushing meaningless papers so he could keep on existing and nothing more. Nothing real at least. He let it die, without thought of starvation or bankruptcy. He just didn't go to work anymore.

He didn't go, because he was too busy preparing.

Jack stood outside of the hidden club, a rose in his hand, and stared up at the sky. The moon rose up, eliminating the stars in its shine. Wisps of clouds drifted across the sky. The city was all around him, each window its own solar system, each building a lonely constellation of the city.

And me, thought Jack. Me wandering with no purpose.

He used a puddle to look into in order to smear on the lipstick, tip the battered top hat just so and straighten the lapels of his tailcoat. And adjusted his carefully made wings.

Tonight's the night, he thought. *Tonight or death.*

The Rosegarden was held in the basement of a union hall, sectioned off with cargo netting on the ceiling and drifting down like a maze. Thousands of tall, tapered candles provided flickering light, standing in bunches in corners and along cramped hallways. The inhabitants ghosted through the darkened ways like shadows of cobwebs. Jack pantomimed their movements by rote, squeezing into eyes shut at times. Thrusting his mind out of his body, becoming one with the movement, his heartbeat rising to the cadence of the beat, his mind one with the distant voice.

He passed the girl with the turned-up collar, bowed to one of the twins and tipped his hat to the boy in the coat and leggings.

He danced mindless on the floor to the beat of the song, contorting his movements to mimic a marionette. He knew Ganit was there, but her eyes upon him didn't bother him in the least. He stopped only to inhale more of his drugs.

He continued long past the time he usually left. And though his body screamed from exhaustion, he kept dancing or quietly, gracefully moving in the shadows.

Endlessly, the night wore on. The music's rhythm became more frenetic over time, losing the voice entirely. If the figures became exhausted, they didn't show. And of course they didn't, after all.

Jack danced on into the night. He danced through the blisters on his feet, swaying slightly he continued.

Wax from the candles began to drip down, pool and collect on the floor.

Ganit approached him, in a taffeta gown and a lace shawl covering her dishwater-blond hair and gave him a nervous look with those plain brown eyes of hers. "What are you doing?" she hissed. Jack danced around her, his eyes alighting on her only momentarily.

The world spun around him, maddeningly, relentlessly. He finally shared a dance with a long-armed girl in torn fishnets and spiderweb tights, her face painted like a Geisha.

He kept exhaustion away chemically, though his body protested. *Bring me closer,* he whispered to his dying body. *Bring me closer to the music.*

He gave a rose to the boy in velvet tights, and whispered into his unhearing ear. He danced on, staggered and twitched, still he danced.

The pace of the music quickened. He heard Ganit shouting to him. *I gave you this,* she shouted, as if in a dream. *I let you escape, so why do you take it so far? Why do you have to go further than I tell you?* Her face looked panicked, torn.

Of course, you can't just escape a little. Once you taste the sky, how can you settle for anything else? You let me out of the maze, Ganit. You showed me something beyond this world. How can I ever willingly walk back?

Jack kept the doll-like smile on his face despite the rising chaos in his body. The air was thick with the smell of burning wax.

The drum beat became more complex, noisier. At any point the music could spiral out of control, yet still it soared higher to a bright and shining zenith. All the figures moved along with Jack in tight circles, their gestures and faces contorted. Their arms reaching, stretching towards the sky.

And the music now a chorus of shrieks and howls, it finally crashed around him as he watched the melting wax figures stumble and fall, the candles guttering and smoking. He stumbled, continuing to dance, the music now mimicking the sound of sobbing from the woman in the corner with a veil over her face, coming out in gasping heaves.

The music choking and trying to breathe, like Jack. The rush is over, he has no more pills, and he's coming down and feeling like everything is underwater or in slow-motion, it's hard for him to breathe. He's choking again, there's water on his face to match the woman's sounds, he trips over the waxen angels half-melted around him . . .

. . . he falls like a rag-doll into a vast ocean he's never seen . . .

. . . he's escaped . . .

Ganit cries until the tears refuse to come, holding the last of the waxen forms to fall, its bleached-out hair and melted wings mix with charred black feathers. The Rosegarden has drowned tonight, but she stays for a little while longer, holding the figure like a mother holds a sleeping son. She cradles it even as the candles gutter out and die one by one, until the mindless labyrinthine city swallows the Rosegarden itself, all its dolls and all its dances.

FADING

KATHERINE HARBOUR

One window of the abandoned house remained unbroken, and the sun at its peak would pass through the Egyptian eye of green and saffron glass to create patterns on the pale walls.

Sprawled on the quilts he'd found in a leather trunk, Jaili basked in the glow.

Dress dummies swatched with cobwebs and boxes crammed with faded, gold-toned photographs surrounded him. He'd set a dozen candles on a table covered with rivers of wax, which had melted into monstrous forms.

He set down his book and sat up, realizing it must be later than he had thought. He had to make his decision soon.

When a flicker of light caught his eye, he flinched, then laughed softly. It was a fragment of mirror in the corner, dusty, but still able to cast back his reflection: a slender boy in thready jeans, t-shirt and hiking boots.

He crawled to the window and rested his arms on the sill scattered with dead bugs. Folding his hands before him, he whispered the small chant he used to change things. Sometimes, he thought, it worked.

He opened his eyes, smoke-green, like the window. Finding everything the same, he sat back on his heels and decided he would do it when he got home.

He would go into the bathroom, run the water and slide the razor across his wrists. Finish it.

Euphoria swirled through him like absinthe and his breath trembled. Glancing down at the delicate scars he'd made before, he stroked them, letting his flaxen hair fall into his eyes. He rested his brow against the cool glass, because, now, everything seemed all right.

The stairs creaked beneath a cautious tread. He listened, not afraid, only curious as to what his last hours would bring.

The attic door opened and a slim boy with long purple-streaked hair stood on the threshold. It was Emery, wearing his old-fashioned greatcoat and leather gloves. A Ouija board was tucked beneath one arm, and his cheeks were flushed with roses of feverish excitement.

"Should we wait 'til the sun sets?" he asked as he trudged in and set the board on a brass-bound trunk. When Jaili shook his head, Emery moved to crouch beside him, considering him from behind the curtain of his black hair. "Hey, Jaili?"

Jaili blinked, smiled. "Let's go out."

They wandered through the park with its sentinel oaks and willows, a green paradise amid ranch houses and swimming pools. Now it was deserted and, but for the scuff of their feet against pebbles and leaves, the silence was complete.

They lay in the grass for awhile and talked about school. Senior year would begin soon. Emery said he'd graffitied one of his racier poems across the back wall of the building.

Jaili grinned his approval. He began to speak quietly of his parents. His film director father and writer mother would be traveling a lot this year. He'd seen the brochures on his father's desk. They had planned for him to stay with his grandparents for the senior year, but he didn't tell Emery that.

He did not tell Emery his plans—that no one would ever have to worry about him after tonight.

Liberated, he rose, pulling Emery up with him. "Let's go downtown. I've got some money."

Filigree Street was a place for browsing, listening to obscure musicians, or rummaging through dark, mysterious shops filled with tie-dye, East Indian silks, strange ornaments and books with peeling leather covers.

Jaili and Emery went rummaging for incense and raspberry wine. Jaili bought a beautiful sheaf of ivory parchment, a quill and ink—for the note. In the dim shop, he saw Emery wistfully fingering a small jade statue of the Hindu god Shiva, and bought it for him.

Outside, the sun was still setting, streaking dusky crimson across the windows of shops and cafes. They found an art gallery reception and sneaked in, thieved things from the buffet table, idly watched the sophisticates, and studied the weird, dark, beautiful paintings on display.

Jaili spotted the artist at once. She looked his age, her hair pink and cut chin-length. Her black velvet dress, ribboned sleeves, black tights and thigh-high boots made her pale skin glow. She wore a Celtic cross on a chain around her neck.

"I like them," he told her, nodding to the paintings.

The artist smiled at him. "They are spirits." She paused. "What a lovely face you have. I'd like to paint you some time."

He lifted his chin. "My name's Jaili."

Her eyes widened. She stepped back, a shadow crossing her face.

Emery was there, leaning against him, warm and taut and smiling nervously at the artist.

"Let's go, Jai. I think they're beginning to catch onto us."

As they left Filigree Street, they passed the stairway to a tall brownstone where a girl and a boy in ripped jeans and velvet shirts were blowing bubbles through plastic wands. The bubbles glittered momentarily in the air, dream-bright. The boy had a sunflower tucked behind one ear.

Jaili breathed in the autumn night, feeling fulfilled, exuberant. He wanted to see the artist again. He thought they could share things . . . and anything could happen. *Everything* could happen.

He closed his eyes and raised a tentative hand to the bruise on his cheek, healing now. He didn't think his father had meant it. The blow had been an overreaction to finding Jaili's small stash of pot. He had never hit Jaili before.

Jaili raised his head, glimmering inside from these few perfect hours. He could do this. He could live and overcome these dark spaces. That was all they were. Sun spots.

Soon, he would have his own place, and he would open up a small shop filled with artifacts and East Indian incense. He could sell the delicate, careful books he created from scraps of fabric, trinkets, his drawings. That was his future. That was what he would do. And he had all of his life with which to do it.

"Where are you going?" Emery asked as Jaili, feeling as if his shoulder blades had flowered with wings, started down the road toward his parents' house,

"Home."

"No." Emery ran after him.

Laughing, Jaili avoided him, smiling at his house, its windows glazed with the last light of day.

"No!" Emery shouted again, and caught him as he set his foot on the flagstones. "Oh, no, Jaili, I told you before—"

Jaili turned to him, smiling. "Told me what?"

Emery's eyes were dark, wild. "You've already done it, Jaili."

Jaili's smile faded.

"Together, remember? In the Old House? We got tired of everything. You had the razor."

And Emery lifted his own wrists, turning them upward so Jaili could see the crisscross of white scars on his friend's pale skin, marring the delicate web of veins. As he stared, they began to bead with blood, and he felt warmth trickling from his own cold skin, over his fingers, from the gaping slashes in his own wrists.

Seeing his face, Emery put his arms around him, and, as Jaili's body began to shudder with sobs, the last of the sunlight faded.

Tomorrow, he would forget again, as he did each time he woke from spirit dreams.

Autumn leaves drifted, whispering, across a deserted pavement.

I didn't mean to. I didn't.

THE BIRTHDAY RITUAL

KURT NEWTON

Birthday.

Danny could hear it in his sleep, like a dream.

Birthday.

In the soft white curtain-light, Danny lay with his head against his pillow, his hands clasped behind his ears. It was still very early in the morning. Too early to "Rise and shine!" Too early to "Wipe the sleepies" from his eyes. So he had to wait, even though the excitement of the day ahead was like sugar in his veins.

Birthday.

Danny gazed at the blue and gold painted horse riding its merry-go-round pole on his dresser top. He liked to imagine it going up and down an' around an' around, but this morning he had other things on his mind. Next to the horse sat a miniature house of mirrored glass. If Danny held it up to the light and looked through the front window, he would see a hundred rooms inside. But Danny didn't feel much like playing with that either. And then there was the fancy tin box that held his tiny treasures, a toy airplane he liked to soar about the room, and a piggy bank filled with coins his aunts and uncles gave him on the rare occasions they came to visit. But none of these held very much interest for Danny. Not even Mr. Bones, a doll made of knots of string and pieces of wood, which hung from the neck of the wall lamp, its feet barely touching the white lace doily below. Not on this particular morning. Because today was Danny's birthday.

Soon the kitchen noises rose up from below . . . the tinkling of a teacup . . . the heavy clunk of a frying pan . . . the sounds of breakfast, of getting up and getting dressed, of Rise and shine! Wipe the sleepies from your eyes! Get up, get up, it's morning time! A new day hides for those to find! A very special day in mind!

Birthday! Birthday! BIRTHDAY!

Danny bounded out of bed and dressed and washed his face and combed his hair all in one swift motion. Then, just as quickly, he grabbed the thick banister and guided himself down the large curving stairway, down to one landing, then another, through the great pools of sunlight beaming in through the curtained windows, until he reached the marbled tiles of the floor below. The first thing he noticed was the blue crepe paper hung in dips across the ceiling. The second was the sign posted on the dining hall entrance that read: *Birthday Boys Beware!* Danny smiled as his stomach bubbled with delight. What else was there? Much more in store to be sure! he thought, and half-skipped down the long hallway to the kitchen and Joseph, the kitchen magician, his only friend in the world.

Joseph was busy slicing vegetables when Danny walked in and hoisted himself up onto the stool by the counter.

"Good morning, Daniel," Joseph said, upon turning around to clear the counter of vegetable scraps, as if he had expected Danny to be there. Joseph wasn't like all the other grown-ups. Joseph's face was more like Danny's own: open and elastic, free to be its own self. Danny felt different around the others. With Joseph he didn't need to pretend.

"Morning, Joseph," Danny replied, spinning around on the stool, half a smile still on his face.

"What will it be this morning?" Joseph asked, his voice the steady, reassuring tone of always.

"Pancakes," Danny chirped.

"Hmm . . . How about something light?" Joseph offered. "Scrambled eggs, perhaps?"

Danny's brow squinted as he thought for a moment.

"Something light and underfilling, so as to leave room for the full day ahead?" Joseph added.

Danny's eyes brightened then, suddenly agreeable.

"Scrambled eggs it is, then!" And Joseph set about working his usual magic right before Danny's eyes.

Danny watched as Joseph selected the proper pan from the many that hung like copper church bells above the countertop. Joseph reached here and grasped there. Eggs were broken; milk poured. Butter sizzled. The whipping whisk was put into action. Joseph winked at Danny as he whipped the egg batter into a foamy white crown. A hiss then followed as the egg batter was transferred to the hot frying pan. Not too hot. The egg batter rose and Joseph tumbled it back in upon itself several times with his wooden spatula, adding a pinch of salt and pepper for good measure.

"A breakfast fit for a prince," Joseph announced moments later when he served the fluffy white eggs complete with English muffin and a tall glass of orange juice, freshly squeezed, to wash it all down.

While he ate, Danny discreetly tried to steer the conversation toward the day's events, but Joseph played his role perfectly, never once letting on. And when Danny's stalling became too obvious, Joseph shooed him away, for "there was much work to be done."

With breakfast now over, Danny set about the task of finding Mother and Father.

Through the big house he traveled, down the long, sun-slanted hallways, past the portraits with the waxwork faces, through empty rooms the size of small buildings, until, at last, he found them both sitting in the sitting room. Father sat behind his morning newspaper, Mother behind the cloud of her cigarette.

"But he's only seven years old!" he heard his mother cry, producing another cigarette cloud, then batting it away as if it were a bothersome moth.

"He'll be eight, and that's old enough," Father said, turning another page of his newspaper.

Danny didn't like the sound of Mother's voice. Why was she so upset? He hesitated by the doorway, his brightness dimming.

"But couldn't we wait another year?"

That's when Father lowered his newspaper and looked across the room at Mother. "Did your mother and father wait another year for you? The world is harsh and cruel, Elizabeth. The sooner he is prepared, the better. The time has come," he said plainly. "Everything will be fine." Father's face was as set and stony as Danny had ever seen it, and Danny quietly backed out of the room before either of them knew he had overheard.

Danny continued on down the hall at a slow, thoughtful pace toward the playroom. There were puzzles in there for him to play with, crayons and building blocks, enough to occupy his time for the rest of the morning.

Mother's worried, a voice whispered inside his head when he reached the end of the hall.

But Father said everything will be fine, he answered back at the intrusive voice.

But Mother's worried, the voice said again, more insistently. And this time Danny didn't answer back; he simply passed through the doorway and into the playroom, and hoped the voice wouldn't follow.

The guests began arriving at noon, aunts and uncles and grandparents from both sides of the family, and people Danny either didn't know or couldn't remember, all in a steady stream of formality. There were bows and hugs and kisses on the cheek, and Danny stood polite and proper as each of them looked down upon him and said things like: "So, this is the birthday boy." Or: "What a fine young man he is." And Danny answered their expressions as best he could read them with smiles of shyness and humble thanks. And soon they were all pooled in a gathering hush around the grand stairway and the entrance to the dining hall, the doors still securely shut.

"Daniel!" Father's voice then called out firmly, and Danny wove his way through the crowd of visitors to the forefront, squeezing past the smells of tobacco and heavy perfume, feeling very small and yet very important, for the time had finally come. He and Father stood face to face for a moment

before Father stepped aside, and, unbidden, Danny pushed through the double doors. What followed then was a loud, joyous burst of applause as the birthday warning tore in two, signaling the start of the Birthday Ritual.

For a moment, Danny couldn't believe his eyes. The dining hall was dressed as he had never seen. The great table was set with the very best of everything: the best china and the best silverware, even the very best crystal glasses from the cabinet Mother always kept locked. And among the dozens of place settings, like huge shiny turtles, the domed lids of a dozen serving trays sat, hiding Joseph's specially prepared birthday dinner. Danny's mouth began to water almost at once. But there was more. Up above the table, the ceiling was decorated with still more crepe paper, and balloons hung from the chandeliers. And off to one side of the hall, a tall white curtain hung suspended in the air, sectioning off an entire area, as if to hide something extra, extra special from Danny's eyes.

The music began then—the trill of a trumpet, the flutter of a flute—and Danny nearly jumped out of his skin when the entire band joined in with one great concussion of metal and bass. It was like every parade imaginable as the guests followed each other in a march toward the great table and the food that awaited them. Mother took her place near the serving end, and Father occupied the big chair at the head of the table. Danny was too busy wondering where the music was coming from to worry about where he should be sitting, until a man dressed like Mr. Bones came rushing over and hurried him along. There was an empty seat next to Mother, and Danny took his place there.

Once seated, Danny looked around and down the length of the great table, over the domed lids of the serving trays and in between the specially folded napkins that stood like candy-colored crowns ready to wear. There was an excited chatter among the guests now that everyone was seated—everyone but Mr. Bones, who had slipped away unnoticed. Perhaps behind the curtain, Danny thought.

When the noise had quieted to a comfortable murmur, Father stood and raised his wine glass to the chandelier overhead, and there was a rush of movement as everyone else did the same. Danny had never had wine before, so he eagerly grabbed the glass before him.

"To Daniel," Father announced, staring down the length of the table at the boy that was his son. "And to the child in all of us."

There were a couple of "hear-hears" in response before everyone brought their glasses to their lips. Danny did the same but closed his eyes as he gulped the deep red liquid, expecting it to taste like medicine. It did and it didn't, and Danny didn't know why he liked it so much, but he did. And when he opened his eyes again the room had grown much brighter. Laughter erupted all around him, for he had emptied his glass while the others still held theirs nearly full. Everyone was smiling so much, Danny thought he could almost see their faces move.

The domed lids of the serving trays were then removed to a chorus of "oohs" and "aahs" as the steam escaped like spirits trapped, and Danny sat back in quiet repose as the wine simmered in his stomach and spread a pleasant numbness that enveloped him like a pair of huge loving arms. This was indeed a day like no other.

Danny ate slowly, for he was too excited to be hungry. Instead, he watched the others as they ate and drank and talked. When his aunts or uncles caught him staring, they would raise their glasses to him in private salute, which made Danny blush. Mother, sitting close, was silent throughout, and Danny noticed the strange way her hands fluttered and sometimes shook the food from her fork. Father ate in a resolute fashion, chewing idly, staring down the length of the table, but looking at neither Danny nor Mother. His gaze fell somewhere between the roasted chicken and the cabbage stew. But, for Danny, there was just too much else to look at and think about to be concerned.

Soon everyone had finished eating and the chandeliers were lit, and the guests who were sitting with their backs to the curtain turned their chairs around. A curious music began to play, and when the moment was right, the tall white curtain rose and there was Mr. Bones again, standing before six of the largest boxes Danny had ever seen. There was a wide ribbon wrapped around each one of them, and each box was decorated in its own unique and colorful pattern. Danny had nearly forgotten that he was the main attraction of the day—the wine having numbed him so—and he sat like all the others, waiting for the show to begin, until Mr. Bones held out his string and wooden hand to beckon him over.

When Danny slid off his chair, it felt to him as though the floor were made of cotton, so light were his footsteps. He joined Mr. Bones in front of the boxes, and Mr. Bones did a clever pantomime with his hands to tell Danny to go ahead.

The lights dimmed and a round spotlight focused all the attention onto Danny's shoulders. The music became a low rattling drumbeat that built as Danny pulled at the wide, colorful ribbon of the first box. The drumbeat snagged when the ribbon snagged. Once. Twice. As Danny pulled, the drumbeat pulled, and for the first time that evening Danny wondered if the music wasn't something that was just in his own head. Finally, the ribbon tore free and the entire front of the box leaned toward him. Danny scrambled out of the way as the box unfolded on all four sides and fell to the floor with a mighty crash of cymbals.

The guests applauded. Again, Danny couldn't believe his eyes. There stood before him a blue and gold painted horse riding a merry-go-round pole, just like the one he had on his dresser top, only this one was six feet tall! And when Danny ran his hand along the horse's flank, it turned its head and regarded him with a quizzical look. Danny was too enchanted to be startled. He almost knew the horse would be real, because he wanted it to be.

Mr. Bones then stood alongside the next box and beckoned Danny again. This time the drum beat without a hitch as the ribbon pulled smoothly and the box fell away. In its place stood a wonderful maze of mirrors in which Danny could see himself six times at once. He was about to investigate the glass labyrinth when Mr. Bones pantomimed that it was time to move on to the next box.

And one by one the boxes fell away to reveal something magical. There was a king-sized treasure chest in which, Mr. Bones demonstrated, Danny could make things disappear. Inside another box was Danny's very own airplane, the size of a bicycle, which operated with the push of a button and flew only as high as the ceiling. And there were money games—number wheels and coin machines—which gave Danny money and then took it back again. Danny was so happy he was almost sad. He had all these wonderful playthings, but there was no one there to play with him.

Mr. Bones beckoned for a final time, for the last of the big boxes remained. And as this box fell away the music rose to a frightful pitch and hung there, and Danny's hair went up on the back of his neck.

Inside this last box was a thick wall of wood, and protruding from its smooth surface, like a carnival game, were the heads and hands of two people: Mother and Father. The music suddenly stopped. Danny was unable to move. Mr. Bones bounded in front of him like a maniacal clown gesturing Danny to proceed. This time, however, Danny didn't know what was expected of him. He stood instead, his feet rooted to the floor.

Mr. Bones then waved for Danny's attention, and slowly, Mr. Bones lifted the wooden mask from his face to reveal to Danny that he really wasn't Mr. Bones at all, but Joseph, the cook, the kitchen magician, Danny's only friend in the world. He had been with Danny all along.

But why would Joseph want him to see Mother and Father displayed in such a manner? Danny thought, his mind racing.

The quiet that surrounded Danny squeezed all the sounds from his body: the tiny drum beat of his heart, the creek of his small joints, even the thick spit at the back of his throat which he had to swallow to keep from choking. Danny suddenly realized what was being asked of him.

With the audience at his back, and the watchful eyes of Joseph at his side, Danny stepped forward into the light until he was almost face to face with Mother and Father. He couldn't tell if they were in pain. He couldn't even tell if they were proud of him for finding the courage to do what it was he was about to do.

He reached up to Mother first, and delicately, like a caress, peeled away the thin layer that covered her face. It was like peeling the shell from a boiled egg, Danny thought—it made a sucking noise as some kind of seal was broken—and underneath, Danny found the face of a beautiful young girl of perhaps ten years of age, who smiled when he smiled, and giggled when he giggled. The removal of the mask seemed to alter her very size, for she squeezed quite easily out of the narrow holes that held her.

It was then Father's turn, and Danny had trouble at first trying to pry the mask off, so stern and set in its place it had become. But it came, stubbornly it came, and finally revealed to Danny what Father was really like beneath all that gruff and grimness.

He was just a little boy, a sad little boy, younger than Danny. Danny guessed the boy's age to be about four or five years old, young enough to have been something like a younger brother. And Danny thought, if given the time, he could teach this little boy a thing or two.

The boy hopped down and joined Danny and the young girl in the spotlight, and the first words they uttered to each other were spoken as if from the same mouth.

"Let's play!" they all said.

At that moment, lights filled the dining hall and music sounded from every corner. To the delight of the guests, who were still drinking their wine and now tapping their feet to the joyous music, Danny and the two other children played as if their hearts were one. They took turns riding the blue and gold painted horse . . . they played hide-and-go-seek in the maze of mirrors . . . they made each other disappear and then reappear from the magic trunk . . . they flew around the dining hall, buzzing over the guests' heads and encircling the chandeliers, in the amazingly small airplane . . . and they played money games and each of them lost, but none of them seemed to mind. And finally, near the edge of exhaustion, they simply sat and ate Danny's birthday cake—which Joseph had wheeled out on a specially decorated birthday cart—and made faces at one another, and laughed until their sides ached and tears ran down their cheeks.

Meanwhile, Joseph kept busy orchestrating the entire affair, and when the evening had grown late, he called Danny over to the great table, for there was one final act left to be performed.

"Announcement," Joseph said in his usual tone, and the guests put their glasses down and gave their full attention. The lights dimmed once again and Danny, now sitting at the head of the table, was bathed in the familiar spotlight. He looked over his shoulder to find Joseph, but Joseph had stepped back and become as unobtrusive as always. Danny looked over his other shoulder to see what his playmates were doing, but they too had disappeared into the shadows. Moments later, though, they joined Danny at the table, only they were no longer the young girl and the little boy. Once again they wore the faces of Mother and Father.

They carried with them a box—a small box, nicely wrapped—and they placed it before Danny's now saddened expression. "Happy birthday, son," they both said, and Danny pulled at the ribbon with caution. When the lid was removed he stared down into the open container for what seemed like a very long time.

With his small hands, Danny reached inside the box and lifted out a perfect mask. It was sturdy and yet thin: the mask of a young man ready to face the world. Danny looked up at his parents and they both nodded.

Danny then closed his eyes and brought the mask close, close enough to feel his own breath against his face. And after taking a moments hesitation to think back, to remember, to catalog every second of this eventful day—the fear and the wonder, the sound of laughter now fading—he pressed the mask firmly against his skin, cutting the flow of tears.

THE LAST POETRY NIGHT AT THE SATURNALIA COFFEE HOUSE

MARK MCLAUGHLIN

I used to go down to the Saturnalia Coffee House every Friday night. To listen to poetry. Occasionally, to read my own poetry. To watch the pretty young things and the not-so-pretty old things mill about, guzzling wine coolers and flavored bottled water. Men and women alike flirted with me. On a scale of 1 to 10, my looks alone would rank me at 6, maybe 7 (I have dark hair and eyes and have been called "ruggedly handsome"). Fortunately, I'm somewhat glib, so my conversation brought my rating up to a firm 8.

The Saturnalia was actually the living room of a run-down mansion, or perhaps I should say mansionette, on top of a wooded hill. The exterior was decked out with fancy trim, but the place was fairly small: two floors (one with four rooms, the other with five) and, enclosed within the gambrel roof, an attic.

The place was owned by Nose: he had a real name (Ambrose, I think), but we all called him Nose because, well, he had a large, thick, ruddy nose with huge pores and little hairs all over it. It looked like a fuzzy baby sponge. He smelled like ointment, too . . . a hospital sort of smell. We were all so rude—we actually called him Nose to his face. He didn't seem to mind. He only smiled and asked if we wanted more raspberry spritzer.

I do miss the poetry readings. Now Nose is dead and the Saturnalia is nothing more than a weed-choked patch of charred boards and bricks.

But I'm getting ahead of myself.

The poetry nights at the Saturnalia were started by my friend Meg, a petite, frizzy-haired bird of a woman who just loved to read her short stories and long, long poems aloud. Her writings usually concerned such topics as her various lovers; her pet snakes, cats, and tarantulas; and her love of the moon and all things nocturnal. Some of Meg's poetry had been published as a chapbook—*Lullabies for Snake Babies*. She had started the readings to promote her chapbook and to give would-be bohemians a fun place to hang out. Every Friday there were two guest poets (friends of Meg, usually) and an open reading. Halfway through the night's festivities, Nose passed a floppy red beret around for donations. "To help pay for the beer," he would say, even though the big, ice-packed tin tub of beverages by the fireplace never included beer.

One night, a newcomer at the Saturnalia caught my eye. He looked to be in his early twenties. He was the palest man I had ever seen. His skin was as white as milk—so white that it was almost blue. His eyes were light green and his eyebrows were practically translucent. His buzz-cut hair glowed with the faintest tinge of cornsilk yellow. His teeth were very small and white and square. His nose was small and flat, like a cat's. His height was about average and he was very muscular. I forget what he was wearing that night, but in the weeks to come, I came to realize that he always wore subdued earth tones.

I watched Pale-Boy out of the corner of my eye. When he laughed, his light-pink tongue touched the tips of his front teeth. He squinted when he smiled, too. At one point, he lit up a cigarette. Several of the poetry night regulars informed him he should smoke outside, so out he went, and I followed.

When we were outside, I tapped him on the shoulder. "Can I borrow a cigarette?" I said.

"You gonna give it back?" he said as he handed one to me.

"Well, no . . ."

"Then you're not borrowing it." He flicked his beige plastic lighter and lit me up. "Sorry. I'm not usually such a smart-ass."

He maintained almost constant eye contact with me as he talked. A good sign.

"How do you like the poetry?" I asked, trying not to cough. He smoked unfiltered cigarettes.

He shrugged and shook his head simultaneously. "I can't really judge. I'm like most writers: I think my stuff's great and everyone else is pumping out shit."

We talked for about half an hour. In that time, I found out that his name was Chad and he worked in a record store. He lived alone in a three-room apartment above a Chinese restaurant. He wrote poetry about vampires, the end of the world, death, loneliness, etc., etc. I was a little disappointed that he didn't ask anything about me.

While we were talking, Chad noticed a little path going off into the trees behind the mansionette. "Let's see where that goes," he said.

I followed Pale-Boy into the woods. I liked the back of his neck: the short hair there formed a light-yellow V pointing down his muscular back. Soon the woods grew too dark for me to see the golden V. Chad was only a light glow of a silhouette, a human aura. He stopped and turned around.

"Here we are," he said, placing his hand on my crotch. "Yep. Here we are." He said that over and over as he opened my pants, as he knelt before me, as he massaged my erection. "Here we are. Here we are." Then he took me into his mouth and could say no more for five, ten, fifteen utterly perfect minutes.

Of course, I returned the favor. I'd had sex with four other men before Chad, and I'd considered all of them generously endowed. But compared to Chad, they were all baby carrot farmers. His erection seemed too huge to be human. For a moment, I was a bit taken aback. But only a moment.

When we returned to the reading, Meg was giving the last poem of the night, as was her way. Chad crossed the room to get a spritzer from the tin tub. I stood by the door. Nose walked up to me and gave me a wink.

"I see you've met my boy," he said.

Panic-stricken, I said nothing.

"Yep, he finally decided to pay the old man's funny farm a visit." He squinted as he smiled. "Oh, I know it seems impossible, an old dogface like me having a little Greek god Apollo for a boy, but it's true." He leaned closer. "You two were gone a pretty long time. Just wanted you to know I don't mind. Nope, not at all. Young people are supposed to have fun."

He winked again, then turned and wandered off. His ointmenty, chemical reek hung in the air.

Chad returned to my side and handed me a wine cooler. "I saw you talking to my dad. What did he say?"

"Nothing, really. He guessed what we'd been doing, but he didn't mind."

"I didn't think that he would." He sighed with obvious irritation, which surprised me.

"What's wrong with that?"

"Oh, it's just that now he's going to be really, really nice to you. Like you're his new kid or something. And that'll probably scare you off." He had a sad, puppyish look in his eyes. "Right?"

"Don't worry. Nose is okay," I said. I studied his Chad's fine pale features. "I guess you take after your mother."

Chad nodded. "Yep. I like men."

During the next few weeks, Chad and I met at movies, restaurants, our apartments, and the poetry readings, where we'd sit next to each other. Everyone knew we were a couple, and it was fun: nobody minded, and since Chad was so very handsome, it made me seem that much more attractive for having snagged him. Nose always made a point of handing me a wine-cooler and chatting with me. When the night grew boring, Chad and I would slip out for a cigarette and a walk in the woods.

Chad started bringing his poems for the open reading segment of the evening. He once gave me a copy of one of his poems, printed in dark red pencil:

HUNGRY FOR YOU

I want to chew on you eat you with
whispering teeth and make you my own
I want to envelop you like a venus
flytrap folding its cold elegant flesh
in upon your tasty smoothness
and so I shall you are mine all mine
you are my delight my love my
sweet surprise my sustenance and
now you are a part of
me

The audience didn't care for his morbid tidbits, and really, neither did I. His poetry did have a certain darkly erotic quality, but frankly, it didn't reflect upon our relationship. I've always had a bit of an ego. I wanted him to write poems about my subtle charms . . . my wit! my broodingly handsome good looks! my finesse as a lover! But then, one doesn't always get what one wants.

Once, while Chad was talking with some poet friends, Meg took his place by my side. "He's gorgeous," she said. "No offense to Nose, but it's hard to believe they share any chromosomes."

"What do you think of his poetry?" I asked.

"Oh, it's all right," she said, rolling her eyes. "I'm not really big on weird scary stuff. What's going on over there?" She nodded toward the other side of the room. Nose had joined the group of poets and even though I couldn't hear what was being said above the noise of the room, I could tell that Nose and Chad were arguing. Chad rushed out of the room and his father followed, shouting and waving his arms.

Meg beckoned to one of the poets—a sandy-haired haiku enthusiast in his late teens named Richard—and he rushed over to us.

"What was that all about?" Meg said.

"Nose doesn't want Chad reading his poetry here any more." The boy said, grinning. It was obvious he enjoyed being in-the-know.

"But why?" I said.

"I don't know!" Richard's eyes grew round. "He just kept saying, 'You know better,' and giving Chad this really poisonous look. I can't believe Chad is being censored by his own Dad."

"It doesn't make sense," Meg said. "I mean, people read about all kinds of stuff here. Acid trips, menstruation, kinky sex . . . you name it. Just last week Daniel read that really long thing about elephants fucking."

"Dads are so lame." Richard nodded knowingly. "My own dad thinks that haiku isn't really poetry because it doesn't rhyme."

He blathered on and on, but I was no longer listening. Somewhere in the house, I could hear, faintly, Nose shouting.

Eventually Chad returned to his seat. His eyes were red and puffy from crying.

"Is everything okay?" I whispered to him.

He shrugged. "I can't talk about it. It's a family thing."

It occurred to me then that I'd never seen Mrs. Nose. "Can I help?" I said.

Chad took me by the hand. Without a word, he led me out of the house and into the woods.

During the next few weeks, I brought up the topic of Chad's mother several times.

His responses to all of my questions were maddening. He always replied in vague sentence fragments: for example, when I asked what she was like, he shrugged and said, "A loner." I couldn't even tell from his responses whether or not his mother was still alive. At his apartment, I asked if I could meet his mother someday and he simply said, "I doubt it." He then began to undo my pants . . . his rather affectionate (and certainly effective) way of saying, *let us please change the subject.*

One Friday night, I showed up at the Saturnalia Coffee House before Chad and everyone else. I found Nose setting out the tin bin of beverages.

"How's the missus?" I said.

He turned and looked sadly at me. His ointment smelled seemed especially strong that day.

"I don't talk about that—" He paused for a split second. "—woman. Don't get on my bad side. You're a nice guy, Brent. I don't mind Chad liking boys and all that. That's fine with me. And it's just as well."

"Just as well?" I could only echo his words, since I had no idea what he meant.

"Well, yeah. Chad ought not to start any families." He began to say something else, then paused, as though rethinking what to say next. "Me and Chad, our relationship is all screwed-up. It wasn't easy raising him. All by myself."

I decided to be persistent. "What about his mom?"

As soon as the words were of my mouth, Nose looked up. Almost involuntarily. Then he looked back at me and said, "His mother is dead. We don't like talking about her."

I thought about what was above us. The second floor? Nose lived up there. Every now and then, he would ask one of the poetry night regulars to fetch something—a corkscrew, or extra glasses—from his upstairs kitchen. The place had piles of newspapers and old clothes scattered everywhere. The third floor? That was the attic. I'd never been up there.

I left Nose to his chores and walked out of the mansionette. Once outside, I looked up at the attic. A dim, slightly bluish light shone through the curtains in the windows.

As I stood there, staring up at the Saturnalia Coffee House, I began to wonder . . . to formulate theories. I *knew* she was up there. Had Nose chopped her up and stuffed her in an old trunk? Was she hanging from a noose, all withered and moldy? Maybe she was still alive but as scary as hell—drooly and white-haired and insane . . .

The poetry folks began to show up. I walked around to the other side of the house, thinking. Was there some way I could slip up to the attic?

A catalpa tree, a bit taller than the house, grew next to the back porch. Several of the branches extended over the roof. A gable window jutted from the side of the roof. Of course, I had no intention of shimmying up that tree . . .

I then noticed that the tree had a makeshift ladder of old boards nailed up along the trunk, leading to the remnants of a treehouse.

I walked into the woods and waited for an hour. By that time, I knew, the poetry reading would be in full swing. There was a full moon out, so I had enough light to see where I was climbing. I ran to the tree and began to climb up the board ladder.

The boards were fairly close together, to accommodate a small child. I pictured an eight-year-old Chad climbing up to the treehouse, and the image saddened me. I felt that the treehouse would have been a place for Chad to hide. From Nose . . . from mean kids . . . or perhaps, from his mother.

I glanced down and even though I wasn't afraid of heights, I had a brief attack of vertigo. I had no idea what I was going to do once I reached the window. Would I be able to get inside? If not, would I be able to get back down the tree? What would I do if I found myself stuck on the roof? Suddenly my mission seemed incredibly foolish. I was risking my neck just to satisfy my curiosity.

"Who's up there?"

The voice came from the base of the tree. I looked down through the branches and saw Richard standing there. He was holding hands with someone, but there were leaves in the way and I couldn't see who it was.

"It's me, Brent," I said.

"You're going to break your neck." This was a girl's voice.

"Yeah. What are you doing up there?" Richard was now talking in a loud stage whisper.

"It's a secret," I said. I leaned out to see who Richard was with (a girl with a partially shaved head . . . very retro-punk) and as I did, my foot slipped and I slid a bit down the tree. My foot caught the next board down, but I still cried out in surprise.

"Oh my God, I think he's going to fall!" the girl cried.

"You wait here," Richard shouted, "I'm going to get Chad." So saying, he ran off to get help, even though I was in no danger whatsoever. I called out for him to come back, but he didn't hear me.

"Are you trying to rip off Nose?" The girl was stage-whispering like Richard. "Can I help?"

I began to climb back down the tree—I didn't want Chad to see me breaking into his father's house. But on the way down, my pants leg caught on something. I looked down, and could dimly make out what was snagging me—it looked like a bent nail.

"He's up there," I heard Richard say.

"Brent! Are you okay?" Fortunately, Chad sounded more concerned than angry.

"Yes, but I'm stuck. I'll be down in a minute."

Chad said, "Thanks, you two. I'll take care of this," and I heard footsteps walking away.

"Are we alone?" I said.

"Yes," Chad replied. "Why were you up in my treehouse?"

"I didn't get that far," I said. I realized then that I could have used the treehouse as a perfectly good excuse for climbing the tree .. .but I had no real desire to lie to Chad. "I was trying to reach the roof. I wanted to look in your Dad's attic."

"Why would you want to do that?" Now Chad sounded frantic. Actually frantic. The tone of his voice answered my curiosity.

"Your mother's in there, isn't she, Chad?"

I heard Chad sigh. Then I heard a rustling in the leaves. The rustling grew closer, closer—and Chad appeared before my eyes. Floating. Floating up through the wide, flapping leaves of the catalpa tree.

"Chad! You're flying!" Now I was the one stage-whispering. He reached over and unsnagged my pants. Then he grabbed me around the chest and pulled me away from the tree. We floated slowly back down to the ground.

"How did you do that?" I looked at Chad's face in the moonlight. He was handsome. Boyish. A little too handsome and boyish. There was something a little . . . artificial? no, but perhaps *surreal* . . . about him.

"If you want to see the attic, I'll take you there," he said. "But we'll use the stairs."

I waited for him to take my hand, but he didn't. He simply began walking. And so I followed him into the Saturnalia Coffee House.

Nose watched us as we walked past the poetry reading. I could feel him watching us as we climbed the stairs to the second floor. Inside Nose's kitchen, Chad opened the bread box and removed a key from between the slices of a moldy loaf of bread.

"Chad? What's going on up there?" Nose was calling from the bottom of the stairs.

"Go back to the poetry reading, Dad," Chad called back. Chad used the key to open a door next to Nose's refrigerator. A smell of dead flies and ointment hit my nose as I looked into the attic stairwell.

Chad flipped on a light switch. The stairs were covered with a thick, shining layer of dried-up dead flies and moths.

Up the stairs we went, insect bodies crunching beneath our feet. The first thing I saw when we reached the top was the couch. It was huge and purple and turned away from the stairs. I looked around and realized that the far corners of the attic were filled with appliances and gadgets. Toasters. Microwave ovens. Food processors. Word processors. A dehumidifier. An old air conditioner. VCRs. Stereos. All of these things were, to some degree, disassembled. At the far end of the attic, I saw a work table loaded with bits and pieces of machines.

Chad took my hand and led me to the front of the couch. "I'd like you to meet my mother," he said.

I looked down at the couch and stared in silence for about ten seconds. And then I screamed.

Chad's mother glowed with a pale blue light. She had an enormous, too-smooth bald head, dominated by the hugest eyes in the world. They were light green, like Chad's. Her mouth was a tiny, red-rimmed slit. She had a small bonelike jut of a nose. Her fingers were probably about seven inches long. Her breasts looked like swirled white rosebuds. Her belly was enormous and her hips were utterly gargantuan. White, slime-streaked slug-tails flapped and twisted where legs should have been. Inset into the folds of her neck and into her armpits and tail-pits were . . . machines. Strange little machines that flashed and whispered and purred. They looked cobbled-together, like pathetic science-fair engines.

That red slit of a mouth opened and a dry whisper wheezed out. "Chad. The friend makes a bad noise. Chad. Make the bad noise stop. Chad."

Chad squeezed my hand hard. So hard that I felt as though I would pass out from the pain. "You're upsetting Mom, Brent," he said. "Cut it out."

Suddenly footsteps thundered on the attic stairs. "Chad," whispered the white couch-thing. "The Love is coming. Chad. The Love is angry. Chad. Make no bad happen. Chad."

Nose came running up to the couch. "What have you done, you idiot, you stupid moron idiot?"

The couch-thing began to float a few inches off of the couch in Nose's direction. "Love. No anger. Love. Make no bad happen. Love." Her dry whisper of a voice was incredibly sad.

She turned and looked at me. I looked back into those huge, moist eyes and felt sorry for screaming. I smiled at her because I could see that she liked me. Her eyes told me everything. These were kind, soft eyes. Loving eyes. She wanted to be my friend. My mother. Perhaps my lover. She wanted to be my everything. I could feel my soul begin to swirl down into the hungry vortex of her eyes. The sensation was indescribably delicious.

"You whore!" Nose's scream startled me, breaking the spell. The white slug-tails were crawling over my lower body. Chad and Nose were pulling the now squealing couch-thing away from me.

"Bad. Me want yummy boy. Bad Chad. Bad Love. Me want. Me want. Bad." The voice of the creature had risen to a shrill squeal. It seized Nose's collar and popped most of his shirt buttons, revealing a hairy chest covered with open sores. The sores appeared to be coated with some sort of brownish grease.

"He's mine, Mom," Chad said with an angry and incredibly odd rumble to his voice. "I just wanted you to look at him. Get your twisties off him. You've already got Love."

"You crummy whore!" Nose slapped the couch-thing across the face. "How many men do you want?"

"Many. Many yummy boys. Bad Love. Many many yummy boys." The couch-thing grabbed Nose by the throat. Nose responded by slapping at one of the many machines scattered on her body.

"Stop it!" Chad screamed. "You're going to hurt her!"

"She's hurting me!" Nose cried. "She started it!" He pounded and pounded at the whirring, flashing engine. Then he reached down and punched at some of the other machines until they shot forth smoke and sparks.

"Bad. Bad. Bad Love. Malfunction." The couch-thing's eyes did the impossible: they bulged even larger.

Sometimes, when I'm having an especially bad time, I'll find myself thinking about the humorous aspects of my situation. It's a sort of kinky reaction to stress, I think. For example: if I'm at a funeral, I'll ponder whether or not the corpse has stiff nipples. At that moment, I thought that the couch-thing's cries seemed to resemble a badly written avant garde poem. As the creature continued to scream, I mentally reformed the words:

"Bad.
Bad Chad.
Bad Love.
Malfunction.
Bad.
Need repairs.
Malfunction.
Need.
Need.
Bad.
Bad Love.

Malfunction.

Malfunction.

Malfunc—"

To this day, I think of the couch-thing's final words as the last poem read within the walls of the Saturnalia Coffee House. It could say no more: pale bile spewed from its lips, choking it. The creature was in a sorry state. Flames billowed from its machines and milky ichor poured from the folds and crevices of its pale bulk. The couch-thing pulled Nose to its breast just as its little engines began to explode, one by one.

I heard sirens outside of the house. No doubt someone downstairs had called the police when I'd started screaming.

Chad threw open the nearest window. Tears streaked down his cheeks as he wrapped his arms around me. We floated out of the window and up into the night sky. We drifted for hours and hours. I didn't try to console Chad. I simply couldn't find the right words. Eventually I fell asleep.

That was ten years ago.

I once asked Chad what his Mom *was* (of course, I phrased my question with a bit more tact than that) and he told me that she was a Saturnian who'd crashlanded on our world, and that Nose had found her and nursed her back to health. When I told him there's no life on Saturn, he said, "Oh? Have you looked?"

Chad and I now live in a farmhouse in the middle of nowhere. We're living off of the insurance money Chad collected after Nose died and the Saturnalia burned down.

The locals don't know about Chad. He started changing a few years back, so I keep him in the attic. I bring him appliances so he can build himself little life-support machines. He seems to know instinctually how to put them together. I let him suck my blood every now and then, and I have to rub a special ointment on the wounds. Chad makes the ointment out of a brownish secretion from a gland on his back of his neck. We joke about that every now and then. He'll hand me a cup of the goo and say, "Just like Mom used to make."

Since he's part Earthling, Chad doesn't look a whole lot like his Mom. His cock is far too big for conventional sex now, but that's okay, because he has grown a few other appendages—and some orifices, too—for my amusement.

What can I say? I adore Chad, and I'll stay with him forever, no matter how he changes.

He is my best friend. My lover. My terror and my delight. You cannot imagine the pleasure he gives me. He is my god. My cosmos. And I understand his poetry now.

Only too well.

HOONEY JEW, HOONEY JEW

STEVE VERNON

And we all need a room of our own, that's what Johnny-Jay had said that the Brother Mick and the Virgin Wolf had said. Hooney Jew didn't really know who the Brother Mick or the Virgin Wolf were, but she figured that they probably made music of some sort because that was all that Johnny-Jay had said he was good at remembering since the magic needle had burnt out most of his brain cells, what ever they were, but that didn't really matter to Hooney Jew anyways, just as long as it was Johnny-Jay who'd said it, because Hooney Jew always liked to hear whatever Johnny-Jay was thinking, and ya, that was good enough for her.

Johnny-Jay had his own room and liked it, too, even though it leaked when it rained, and the walls turned to mush, like Hooney Jew's morning bowl of cereal. Johnny-Jay always said that he never needed a real room anyways because a real room would close him in and shut him up and Hooney Jew knew what that was like, ya for sure.

Hooney Jew liked Johnny-Jay, even if he couldn't think too good, and even if she had only met him three weeks ago, because he was nice to her and didn't yell or break anything. Poppa always would get too mad and break things and then lie about it and say that they were accidents, and that they had broken themselves when they hadn't really, and saying things real loud like what the hell did he ever do to deserve, and if I ever get my hands and Jesus Christ, poppa must have been a real close friend of Jesus Christ because he was always talking to him that way, and he wished to hell that he could get away from this whole fucking mess, that was poppa's word for family, a whole fucking mess, and Hooney Jew, Hooney Jew.

It was poppa who'd first given her the name Hooney Jew, he'd say aw Hooney Jew, even though she wasn't one of those like the Goldsteins next door, but poppa always had a hard time with his whys because his poppa had come from an island called Puerto Rico, poor bleeding Puerto Rico poppa would always say and thank Christ he was out of that whole fucking mess and Hooney Jew thought that maybe that meant that poppa might have left another family back there too.

Hooney Jew knew her name wasn't always Hooney Jew and sometimes after poppa had gotten too mad at her, momma would talk to Hooney Jew in a whisper that was kind of nice and not so nice to hear and she'd call Hooney Jew Catherine or Kathleen or Katie because even momma wasn't really sure anymore and couldn't remember so good, maybe because of her bottle, or maybe because of poppa getting too mad at her too many times.

But Hooney Jew would never cry, even when the teacher had told momma that Hooney Jew would have to be held back again, even though she was old enough for a really high school, and maybe they should think of sending her to a special school for children like her, but that costs money poppa would say, and so Hooney Jew stayed at home, because she was dumb just like poppa said, and momma had held her and rocked her and had said don't cry baby, darling, momma's special one, but Hooney Jew had stopped crying long ago and anyway it was momma who had held all of the tears.

Hooney Jew was her momma's special one, because her momma had told her so. Her with her bright red hair and green speckled eyes like snake's eggs, so her poppa would know that she wasn't his, momma said, and poppa would get too mad and kept on trying to prove that she was his, and getting too mad again and again because he couldn't do it. She was momma's special dream, her momma would say, and the Martians had made her because one of them had come to her momma disguised as a door to door salesman and that's how Hooney Jew was made. Poppa would always say aw you lying bitch to momma, and then he'd get too mad again but momma kept saying that one day real soon she would sell her story to the *Enquirer* or maybe *People*. Momma said that they print stories like that all the time and that someday real soon she'd get paid good money so she and Hooney Jew could say good-bye to poppa, but right now she couldn't because she was a little afraid that they would laugh at her and call her an old rummy, although Hooney Jew never saw her momma playing any cards. Momma was also afraid that something inside her might break like the time poppa had got too mad at momma too hard and momma had to go to the hospital and Hooney Jew had to tell the men a lie that momma had fallen downstairs herself.

The memory of momma lying there on the floor at the bottom of the stairs with her left leg bent backwards and around like Hooney Jew's favorite dolly after poppa had picked it up one too many times made her think mad thoughts and she decided she hated poppa even if he'd been sorry afterwards, even more sorry than he'd been after the rat had bit Hooney Jew on the ear.

That had been in her room, the one that poppa sent her to when ever he got too mad. She usually slept on the floor, sometimes in the hall, some-times in the kitchen, and sometimes by the door when it was too hot and she needed a draft of cool air. But when poppa would get too mad she would have to go sleep in her room.

Momma and poppa always slept on a mattress in the TV room, even though the TV didn't work anymore since poppa had kicked his sneaker into it after his favorite team had lost. The mattress had two broken springs in it that poppa would turn towards the floor and sometimes when she was in her room she could hear the springs going squeak squeak like rats and Hooney Jew would get a little scared and then she'd hear momma moaning and saying make me a baby over and over which was silly because momma was a grownup and besides she had told Hooney Jew that the Martians had broken her so she couldn't make any more babies, and then poppa would make a funny sort of groan and the squeak squeak would stop and after that she would always hear the snap of poppa's shiny steel lighter.

Poppa was always very proud of his lighter and would always brag to whoever would listen that it had been his poppa's lighter in the war, but momma had told Hooney Jew once that yes Granpa had been in the war but poppa had really bought the lighter in a surplus store and that poppa sometimes liked to tell stories.

Hooney Jew knew that already. Sometimes before bedtime poppa would sit in the kitchen on the high backed chair that made his back feel good and smoke his cigarettes and blow smoke rings to make Hooney Jew laugh. Sometimes he would tell stories of poor bleeding Puerto Rico, and how his poppa had come to America to find freedom, and had fought and died in their goddamned war. With poppa it was always a goddamned war, as if he were mad at it. And then he would tell her how he had to find work on a fishing boat as a small boy to help feed his family and how he had met his momma in a fish market and how he remembered how badly they both had stunk. That part always made Hooney Jew laugh whenever poppa told it.

Hooney Jew never really cared how much of poppa's stories were true or how much of them were made up, because they made her happy and when he told them to her it was the only time that Hooney Jew could ever really remember loving her poppa. Afterwards he would turn out the light and tell her to go to sleep, and when she would say she couldn't sleep he would sing to her a song that his momma had sung to him when he was just a very little boy until Hooney Jew finally did go to sleep.

In the winter Hooney Jew always slept in the kitchen next to the stove and when she could she would turn on the gas in the stove just a little bit just to try and keep warm but then poppa would yell and say don't you know that gas costs money and Hooney Jew anyways, and then Hooney Jew would turn off the stove before her poppa would get too mad and send her to her room and she would pull the old kitchen ragrug over herself to try and keep warm.

Hooney Jew used to sleep in the bathtub and make a little bed with the towels, always being especially careful to fold them up in the morning so that poppa wouldn't get too mad at her. She'd pretend that she was a fairy princess or maybe a Martian queen in a shiny white castle but then poppa started coming in and doing his things in front of her and that spoiled everything and besides it smelled too bad and so she'd stopped trying to sleep in the bathtub.

She often wished she could run away and live with Johnny-Jay, but he said she couldn't because he lived in a large cardboard carton in the back of an alley, two streets over, and after a few rainy spells Johnny-Jay would need to look for a new place to live because the old one would be melted away, just like the witch in the movie she used to like to watch, before the TV stopped working.

Hooney Jew didn't care about all that and would have gone and lived with him anyways, but Johnny-Jay said no, and she hadn't argued with him because she was always afraid that Johnny-Jay would get too mad at her just like her poppa and then he would tell her to go to her room like poppa always did and that would spoil everything.

Whenever poppa got too mad at Hooney Jew he would make her go under the floor, and she would have to lift up the loosened floor boards in the hallway and then poppa would tell her to go to her room and then he'd laugh, and he would sometimes get too mad again and say go on Hooney Jew and so she'd go on in and poppa would cover her up with the floor boards and then the bugs would find her and crawl on her and once a rat had bit her and she'd tried not to scream but in the morning when momma saw what the rat had done to her ear then momma had screamed and then poppa was sorry for a while and tried not to get too mad and Hooney Jew had never listened very well since then.

That was why when poppa said that he was really something to Hooney Jew last week she had thought that maybe she hadn't heard him right or maybe his accent was acting up because even though she looked really hard she couldn't see any horns on her poppa anywhere, but then poppa asked her to do something that she didn't want to do but she did it anyways because she was afraid poppa would get too mad and afterwards it was all sticky inside and poppa had said now you are a real woman but Hooney Jew just felt dirty and not right and had to take a bath for a long time before she almost felt better.

Afterwards poppa had sat up on the floor beside her and snap went his shiny steel lighter and he had smoked his cigarette and had even seemed a little sorry about what he had done but Hooney Jew knew that this was going to become a thing that poppa did, like getting too mad, and so she had her bath and then got dressed and then had gone out to find Johnny-Jay who always knew the right things to say when things were all too wrong.

But when she found Johnny-Jay he was all excited and said that it was a good thing that she had come when she did and that he was going to be leaving soon because winter was coming on and he would have to go. That was when Hooney Jew had asked Johnny-Jay to marry her. At first Johnny-Jay had thought this was Hooney Jew's way of making a joke and he had laughed, but then she had asked him again, harder. Then Johnny-Jay did a funny thing. He grew really quiet and stroked her hair like her poppa sometimes did when he was telling her one of his stories, and then Hooney Jew knew that Johnny-Jay was going to tell her no.

But first he told her a story about a girl he had known when he was as young as Hooney Jew, which seemed a strange thing to say to Hooney Jew, because she had never thought of Johnny-Jay being much older than her poppa, even if his hair was turning gray. Johnny-Jay told her that he'd lost that girl a long time ago, back when he'd first tried using the magic needle and Hooney Jew said that if they got married then they could go and look for her together and it would be easy to find her, like the time momma had lost her radio, and momma and Hooney Jew had looked all day and found it under the floor boards, broken, in Hooney Jew's room and momma had gotten too mad at Hooney Jew for the very first time and had thrown her empty bottle against the wall behind Hooney Jew's head, and even though Hooney Jew had said she hadn't touched momma's radio, momma had just said o you lying bitch and hadn't listened to anything else Hooney Jew said.

Johnny-Jay got very quiet for a while and then he cried for a while and he said that Hooney Jew would have to find somebody else. Hooney Jew didn't know who else that somebody else could be, because she didn't know anybody else who was lost. Johnny-Jay said that he couldn't marry her because he was too old and he just couldn't be with a woman in that way since the magic needle had ruined him and Hooney Jew hadn't been very sure what he'd meant by that way but she'd gone away like he'd asked her because she didn't want to make Johnny-Jay cry, because he might get too mad or something.

And then she had gone home and poppa had got too mad at her like nothing had ever happened between them in the morning, like they hadn't done the thing, and he'd said go on Hooney Jew and she had cried a little for the very first time in a long time and she said in a very small voice ya who needs me and she had gone to sleep in the kitchen and turned on the stove just a little because she was suddenly cold and winter was coming on and poppa had yelled turn that off and gas costs money don't you know and she said ya Hooney Jew and had turned off the flame but left the gas running and had gone to her room without waiting to be told to.

Poppa didn't bother to come cover her up with the floorboards, and she couldn't do it herself, so she just lay there staring up at the ceiling, listening to momma and poppa and the springs squeak squeaking and for the first time she knew what they were doing and she wondered why her momma did the thing because it didn't really feel good and she was getting really sleepy and she thought she could smell something and then she was just about to close her eyes and maybe dream about her and Johnny-Jay running away and getting married down south, when she thought she heard a voice saying it's time to go now and then she heard the very loud snap snap click of poppa's shiny steel lighter and then . . .

PALE FRUIT

JEFFREY THOMAS

The woman who opened the door in answer to Griffin's knocks was beautiful, and it was this—more so than the fact that she was most certainly not the person he had expected to greet him—that made him falter speechless for several beats. Her hair was long and straight, that drab shade of watery brown that was really like no color at all, but it was parted in the center and framed like curtains an oval face of great impact. The strange woman's mouth was decadently plush, lips that had been stung by the whole hive of bees held compressed into a solemn pout. They glistened a moist and glossy crimson, some swollen exotic fruit. Her eyes had a feline shape and were of a blue that was clear almost to the point of transparency. Too much mascara only heightened the effect.

"Yes?" the woman, surely only a girl of eighteen or nineteen, asked him at last in a dark, vaguely surly voice.

"I'm sorry . . . um . . . I was looking for my landlord . . . uh, Guy?"

"Guy Hamlin," the young woman droned.

"Yes. Guy Hamlin."

"I'm Guy's daughter, Idelia."

Griffin smiled. "Do you call your father by his first name?"

Just that lynx-like stare for a moment or two, and then, "Yes."

The girl—Idelia Hamlin, then—was small and obviously very slender, lost like some dour, doleful child in her over-sized sweater. Black tights clung to legs almost alarmingly thin, and her bony feet were bare, the red polish on their nails flaking away like old blood. The dim bulb beside the door glowed on her high forehead, and made her pallid, translucent flesh seem almost softly luminous. Normally Griffin did not care for the starving model look, that heroin chic, the anorexic waif that was the current ideal, as dictated by the media. His interest lay in substantial women, voluptuous, large-breasted, round-bottomed. His ex-girlfriend Natalie had been plump as a Renoir nude. This girl was anything but substantial. And yet, those ice-blue eyes, the too-ripe painted lips that seemed to overcompensate for the rest of her, pinned his heart like a struggling, dying moth inside his chest.

He might have disbelieved her about being Guy's daughter, except that Guy also had uncanny blue eyes, if not of quite so light a shade. Yes, he could see Guy in her unsettling gaze. But otherwise there was no similarity, as Guy was singularly unattractive and a good four hundred pounds, Griffin wagered. Oh yes . . . Guy. He had come upstairs to see Guy. Griffin realized he'd been mutely staring again.

"I'm Griffin Shores; I live downstairs. Is your father home? I have the rent . . . and some books to return." He held them up as proof. "He lent them to me."

Idelia gazed at the books in his hand, and seemed hesitant or indecisive as to what to do next. But finally she said, "Why don't you come in, then." She held the door wide for him. Before that, she had been blocking it warily with her thin frame.

"Okay, um, thanks." Griffin slipped past her, lightly brushing against her sweater. Very consciously, he inhaled as he did so, and stole a furtive whiff of her musky perfume.

"What are the books?" Idelia asked as she turned away from the door.

"Oh, about the supernatural, the occult, mostly," Griffin replied with some degree of embarrassment, as if caught with a stack of pornography. "Your father and I got to talking one day, and he found out I work in a book store and love to read. He's pretty enthusiastic about these books . . . he thought I'd find them interesting, too."

Idelia nodded absently, but said, "I think they're dangerous."

"Books?"

"Those books."

"Oh. Well, ah, so . . . 'is Guy here?"

"No. He isn't. He's away."

So why had she let him in, he wondered, when she could have just accepted the books out on the landing? There was something in her spacy manner that suggested drugs, or even a psychological problem, or both—not that it decreased his lust by much. "Um, so when will he be back?"

"Not sure. Not soon." She shrugged vaguely. "If you don't feel comfortable leaving the rent with me, you can wait until he returns."

Griffin didn't feel comfortable with that, so he changed the subject. "I didn't know Guy had ever been married." He didn't add that his impression had been that Guy was a very lonely—bitterly lonely—man, who had never had a girlfriend in his life, let alone a wife with the kind of genes to produce a creature like this one. Also, he had taken Guy to be only in his mid thirties; he must have sired Idelia when quite young.

"They're divorced," Idelia explained. "My mother lives out of town. I'm just visiting here."

"I see. Then I'll bet you haven't been to the store where I work. It's just down the street—'Book Plates'? We have a little coffee shop in there. If you're not busy, maybe I could buy you a cup of coffee and a piece of pie?" His throat clicked as he swallowed a phlegmy glob of nervousness.

"Outside?" Idelia glanced rather suddenly at one of the windows in this front room, a parlor. Ancient, water-stained paper of a dark color covered the tenement apartment's walls, and all the curtains were drawn, all the shades pulled. "No—thank you."

Griffin felt like he'd totally humiliated himself, as usual. He called the look women gave him when he asked them out "the tarantula." As if, instead of asking them out, he had extended his open palm with a tarantula on it. He had gotten along with Guy, evasive as Guy was (this was the first time Griffin had actually been inside his apartment), not only because they shared a passion for books, but because they were both unlucky bachelors. Well, he had had Natalie, and Guy had had his wife, so there was always hope for the future . . . and Griffin felt he was at least more attractive than Guy, though that wasn't saying much.

"Well, I've got to start my shift in a half hour, anyway, so I guess I should be going. You should drop in some time, though—I mean, just to look at the books. It's a nice little place."

Idelia said nothing in reply; just stared at him, as if to hypnotize him. He was hypnotizing himself, he thought, and he'd better break off; he was starting to feel light-headed just being in her aura of subtle perfume and glowing flesh.

And then, she took two steps to cross the space between them, to float toward him like a somnambulist, and her arms drifted up to him, the sleeves of the bulky sweater sliding back to reveal the thinness of her arms, and her hands alighted on either side of his face, her touch so soft it was like smoke, but cold smoke. A question half rose in Griffin but before he could give it sound, her face too floated toward him, and she pulled his face down and pressed that luxuriant mouth against his.

He put his hands on her arms, as if to push this stranger away, but her tongue slipped into his mouth, cool and anxious, and he found his arms sliding around her instead, to press her whole body to him. He could almost have wrapped his arms around her twice; he was accustomed to Natalie's broad back, her warm cushions of flesh. This bird-like body with its sharp points of bone and its insubstantial lightness was alien to him. But that alienness of her body and of her actions increasingly stimulated him. He pushed his own tongue into her mouth in turn, and grew aroused, grew desperate to enter her down there as well . . .

Her hands had moved from his face down to his waist, and now slid under his own sweater and the shirt beneath to the bare skin. She began to bunch the material in her hands as if to pull it off him, over his head, and this caused him to open his eyes in surprised desire.

Her eyes were open, too, perhaps had been open all along, and right there in front of his own—so blue, so intense, so very hungry that they frightened him. But it wasn't just her hunger that suddenly disturbed him. Again, he had been reminded of Guy's eyes. It was as if Guy had changed form so as to seduce him, but had just now dropped his defenses to reveal himself lurking beneath the mask. It was, Griffin thought later that night when mulling over these events, a ridiculous idea. Had Guy lost three hundred pounds in the two weeks since Griffin had last seen him, and undergone a sex change operation to boot? But the girl was, of course, a part of Guy, being his daughter—a physical extension of him.

She must be insane. Why would she try to seduce him, a stranger? He was hardly irresistible, he was the first to admit. He thought himself as bland and colorless as a ghost. So why this frantic passion? Yes, she had to be disturbed, and however beautiful she was, that knowledge began to repulse Griffin, and he stepped backwards away from her.

But she clung to the bottom of his sweater, walked forward with him. "Look at me," she breathed. "Look at me. Want me. Want me to be here . . ."

Increasingly unnerved, Griffin had to actually take hold of her bony wrists and extricate himself as gently as he could. He gave a very nervous chuckle, embarrassed and horrified for the both of them. "I'm sorry, Miss Hamlin, but I have to go to work now. I'm sorry." He turned quickly to the door, let himself out into the hall, at any moment expecting the woman to pounce upon him to drag him back . . .

But she didn't, and when safely through the threshold Griffin threw a look back at her. She remained standing where she had been, her eyes on him but seemingly having lost their focus. Huge empty eyes, eyes of a lost child, their color drained from them, and her lipstick smeared across her cheek like blood.

"It's okay," she told him. "It's for the best anyway, if I go away. For the best . . ."

He faltered, and repeated, "I'm sorry." He didn't know what else to say. And then, he started downstairs. Above him, he heard the door quietly snick shut.

Fallen leaves scrabbled across the sidewalk like large insects that took flight, swirled briefly, settled to earth again. The leaves were dark red and soon to crumble, flakes of crusted blood drifting down from the dying sun. This sanguine orb made deep blue-purple silhouettes of the old houses along the street, narrow and huddled close together against the chill and seeming to lean over Griffin as if to box him in.

He gave a little shiver, wishing he'd brought his jacket with him, but as he'd related to Idelia, the book store was just down the street and around the corner. During the week, he worked first shift hours, but on Saturdays—as now—he was scheduled from evening 'til closing. He had no social life to sacrifice.

He could still feel Idelia in his mouth; she had seemed more solid there than in his arms, where despite her craving she had been so wispy and brittle. Thinking of her made Griffin dart a glance back over his shoulder at the house he shared with his landlord . . . a glance up at the second storey.

Perhaps he had sensed a gaze upon his back, for someone was indeed gazing down at him from an upper window. He stopped, and squinted, realizing that it was more than one person. Again, the buildings were murky with the sun dropping behind them, and there was no light on in that upper room, but he thought he could see three or four figures framed in the glass, crowded close together as if all of them pressing to get a look at him. His impression was that they were naked, all of them, but whether they were male or female it was difficult to distinguish. What he did seem to observe, however, was that every one of the pallid figures was wasted to cadaverous thinness, and splotched here and there with inky darkness as if someone had camouflaged them with black paint. These must only have been darker shadows than the rest of the gloom, but Griffin had no further opportunity to tell, for the figure closest to the front drew down the shade, and blocked them all from view.

Griffin remained staring at the window for several moments, as if the shade might be lifted again, but it wasn't. Did the figures continue to peek at him, however, around its edges?

He decided he must have been mistaken. It must have been only one person, and that must have been Idelia. She had disrobed, and exposed herself, hoping to entice him back, but then had thought better of it. Yes, it could only be that.

Griffin turned back toward his destination and picked up his pace, anxious to be out of this dark side street before it closed in on him altogether.

As he lay in bed that night, staring up at the black pool of his ceiling, he thought of the woman who was staying upstairs from him, even now perhaps in the room just above him.

Why was she visiting, if Guy were away elsewhere? To housesit in his absence?

Tonight, at work, Griffin had attempted—without success—to locate the various books that Guy had lent to him and which he'd returned to Idelia. He thought he might like to peruse them further, after all. He had been thinking about some of the pages Guy had turned down the corner of, or tagged with a scrap of paper as a bookmark, passages he had highlighted with a yellow marker.

One story which Guy had obviously been drawn to related how a group of Canadian researchers of the paranormal, headed by a Dr. George Owen, had in the 1970s invented a ghost. They had concocted for him a spurious history, and the name of Philip, using the seance form as a way to focus him into being. Eventually, he apparently took on his own life, or after-life, and contacted the researchers as if he had been a real ghost. As if, Griffin thought, there were real ghosts.

Philip had communicated through rapping, and had even made a table physically "dance" about a room.

Another story that had particularly seemed to impress Guy was represented in several of the books; it discussed how the author Alexandra David-Nell, while studying in Tibet, learned how to create something called a *tulpa,* a thought form given its own sort of life through intense and lengthy concentration. Her *tulpa* was given the identity of a monk, who after a time was even physically seen by another person and mistaken for a man of flesh and blood. This monk was at first benign in aspect, but after a while grew strangely sinister even in his appearance, and took on his own life to the extent that David-Nell felt he was shrugging off the yoke of her power over him, like a child outgrowing its parents and rebelling for independence. David-Nell had then struggled for half a year to "unmake" him.

An almost subliminal sound broke into Griffin's thoughts. It was the squeak of a loose floorboard in the room above him. He realized after several moments that he was holding his breath, as if even that sound might prevent him from hearing a repetition of the stealthy creak, but no more came.

His ceiling, lost in blackness, seemed suddenly not to be there at all. He imagined it was a gaping opening, and he imagined a figure was up there at the edge of the opening, gazing down at him, waiting for him to fall asleep. Watching, in the dark, with eyes of too light a blue.

Griffin reached for the lamp on the night stand, almost toppled it in turning it on. His ceiling returned, white and solid, if the plaster a bit cracked.

He fell asleep with the lamp still on . . . but dreamed of multiple sets of pale blue eyes peeking at him through those cracks in the plaster.

On Sunday, Griffin put on a jacket and set out to get a paper and a coffee-to-go at his place of employment (couldn't even stay away on his day off, he chided himself), but found himself getting no further than the front hall, where he gazed up the stairs that ascended into the gloom of the second floor landing.

He wondered if he should apologize for rejecting Idelia Hamlin's advances yesterday evening. He could tell she'd been hurt, dejected. She had said something like it being for the best, anyway. Something about going away. Going back home, wherever that was? Would she have already left?

More than this, however, he wondered if he should have rejected Idelia Hamlin's advances at all.

In the light of a new day it was difficult for him to imagine how he could have been so uncomfortable with her little . . . show of affection . . . that he would have broken off from it. It was he who was mad, not her. Here was this gorgeous fragile flower of a young woman, certainly no older than twenty, who had thrown herself at him, an undistinguished-looking man in his early thirties who had had fewer lovers in his life than his sixteen year old nephew had, he reckoned. Well, that must be it right there, then. He was too inexperienced to respond to spontaneous desire. Too timid. Had he not been so bloody meek all his life, he might have been more experienced by now. Have a lover right now rather than be living alone. Own a book store rather than work in one. He stood mired in his self-disgust—but his fingers had been curling around the railing of the staircase.

As if pulling a boot from sucking mud, he placed his right foot on the first step.

In the murk of the upper hall the door was an obscure portal almost indistinguishable from the shadowy wall. He rapped upon it. A timid knock, despite his new determination. Watch it be Guy who opens the door, he thought. Guy's great bulk, and Idelia having fled away like some nervous fawn, back into the deep woods . . .

The door opened, and it was Idelia who stood in the threshold.

She wore the same heavy, dark brown sweater and black tights as yesterday, her feet again bare, but she had wiped away her dramatic red lipstick and the dark mascara. It left her looking even more pale, if this were possible, white almost to bloodlessness, and made her eyes look more vulnerable, her too-full lips tender and more child-like. She appeared more sad than surly, as when she'd answered his knock last evening.

"Hello," she murmured.

"Hi. Um, I'm glad to see you're still here. I just, ah, just wanted to . . . I hope yesterday I didn't hurt your feelings . . . you know . . ." He chuckled quite uneasily, threw up one hand. "I didn't mean to run away like that and . . . embarrass you or anything . . ."

The young woman looked away and smiled slightly—half bashfully and half bitterly, he felt—and then looked back at him, her smile fading away again, that brooding drowsiness returning. "Why don't you come in?"

"Yeah, sure," Griffin said, trying to sound casual while an almost nauseous passion loomed up through his guts like a solid invading object. It was as though he were penetrating himself. "Okay . . ."

As soon as Idelia had closed the door behind them and turned to face him, she reached beneath the hem of her sweater and slipped her thumbs under the rim of her tights, began skinning them down her legs like a snake shedding its skin. The contrast of the slender snowy limbs that were revealed from behind the eclipsing black material was shocking and mesmerizing. She balled the garment and tossed it onto a chair and then stood staring at him expressionlessly. She didn't remove her over-sized sweater, so that it reached to the tops of her thighs and hid her private area in delicious secrecy.

She extended her hand to him. He took it, and it was small and cool, and she led him to the bedroom. Like a sleepwalker he followed, no longer questioning or protesting.

"I thought I'd starve myself," she told him as she crawled onto the large bed which Griffin felt must be Guy's. "I thought that was for the best. To just let myself fade away." She stretched onto her back, still in her sweater, but pulled it up just enough for him to catch a shadowed glimpse of soft hair. "But now here you are," she went on. "Here you are. I leave it all up to you. My own will . . . it isn't like yours . . ."

Her words trailed way, but Griffin wasn't listening, at any rate. He began to pull off his jacket, fumbled with his buttons. He watched her white, slim legs part like a flower opening its petals.

As soon as he was above her he was inside her, and she hooked her heels over the backs of his legs. He clamped a ravenous mouth over those tender lips as if to willingly bruise them, held her skull between his trembling hands. But she pushed at his shoulders gently, broke their kiss and gazed up at his face. Now she held his head between her palms.

"I want to see your eyes," she breathed huskily, shakily. "Look at me. Don't close your eyes. Look at me . . ."

He did as she asked. In his fevered state, it was the best he could do for her in the way of foreplay. But he awkwardly kneaded her small left breast through the heavy material of her sweater . . . and then reached his hand to its hem so as to slip beneath it and touch the bare flesh of her belly, her nipples that must be as pale a pink as her lips . . .

She suddenly reached to stay his hand from sliding under her sweater. "Don't," she whispered. "Please . . ."

"What's the matter?"

"I'm—too thin. I'm embarrassed."

"You're lovely. You're so lovely. You don't have to worry. I want to see you . . . please . . . I want to touch you, Idelia." He braced himself higher above her, still deep within her, and took hold of the sweater's edge. Her hand was still closed on his wrist, but her grip was either weak or fatalistic, and he peeled back the sweater to bare her upper body. He wanted to taste it. He wanted to lose himself in its pale glow . . .

But it was not pale beneath her sweater. There was a shadow there, glaringly black against the contrasting whiteness.

A patch of liquid darkness like an inky stain covered much of the woman's belly, starting just above the squint of her navel and encompassing the lower half of her right breast, nicking the bottom of her aureole. It was not a hole, in that its edges blended into the flesh, and yet it was of a more profound depth than any hole. It was as though the void of space itself had burned through her thin tissues. And in this oblivion, a mist or fog rose and fell in billowing, blowing and soundless waves.

"You want to see me? You want to touch me?" A membrane of tears began to jiggle across her wide eyes. "Touch me." She still held his wrist, and drew his hand toward that dark window.

Griffin yanked his hand free of her, slipped out of her (what darkness had he been penetrating within her?) and backed naked across the room. He didn't want to know what that blackness felt like. Whether he would meet with solid flesh, or whether his hand would slip through her into that cold, churning mist.

She slung her legs over the edge of the bed, pulled the sweater down again to hide her wound, if such it was. "It's spreading," she informed him. "Every day . . ."

"What are you?" Griffin managed, in something like a whispered sob. "A ghost?"

Rising, Idelia smiled. "Not even that. A ghost at least was once alive."

She was too near the door, but there was another on his left. She took a step toward him, still smiling, still weeping, and he darted to his left without waiting to gather his clothing. He plunged into another room, slammed the door, but could find no lock. He turned his back against it to see where he was. It was another bedroom, with no lamp on, just dim sunlight that struggled through the drawn shades and closed drapes. But against this wan light, a figure shuffled into silhouette. Then another. Shadows rustled now to both sides of him. Griffin whirled around and flung open the door he had just come through . . . but of course, Idelia was there, and he backed helplessly into the center of the room.

She flicked on a wall switch, and an overhead light came on. Griffin found himself ringed by a half dozen people. At least, they were people to varying extents.

They were all women, and all naked, but tainted as Idelia was with that plague of darkness. More afflicted than she, in fact. They were more skeletal, as well—cadaverous. One woman had no breasts left whatsoever, and one of her arms had vanished at the shoulder, where the black void gaped. Another woman had an abyss where her face should have been, this mask of nothingness framed in long straight hair like Idelia's. One woman had no head remaining at all, but her body still stood at attention. Well, she was a kind of machine, wasn't she? A machine Guy had made from the ether. That was it, wasn't it?

"These are my sisters," Idelia said. "They came before me. They were sketches, mostly, though Guy still used a few of them."

One of them—the very first?—was not even fully in focus. She looked like a badly blurred moving figure in a photograph, though she stood quite still before him.

And what of Guy? Griffin had no doubts about a great hulking form on top of the bed. It was wrapped in a blue plastic tarp, and this package wound with silver duct tape. There was a faint smell of rot which he had first, erroneously thought was coming from the decaying women. How long Guy had been dead and how he had died were the only particulars that needed answering. Idelia noticed his frantic glance at the bundle.

"We didn't kill him, if that's what you think. We aren't vampires. He had a heart attack, I think. Three of us were with him." She tittered, her lower lip quivering. "It's funny, isn't it? We with too little flesh, and he with too much? He couldn't survive the pleasures he wanted. He was too hungry. And here we are, with no life, and we outlive him."

Griffin looked back at Idelia. "Don't hurt me," he whimpered.

"You aren't listening," she laughed, then she sobbed, and gestured at the bulk on the bed. "I loved him, you know. We all did. He made us to love him."

Griffin began to edge closer to her. She, at least, he knew somewhat. The others, however much they looked like her, were too silent, and too ghostly. But she was right; even phantoms were more substantial.

"Please, Idelia," he said, "just let me go."

She looked at him abruptly, then stepped back from the door. "I wouldn't stop you, Griffin. I told you, this isn't about my hunger—it's about yours."

He slipped through the door. She made no attempt to follow him, merely watched him from the adjoining room, along with those of her waning sisters who still possessed eyes. He dressed hurriedly, not taking his eyes off her . . . Guy's daughter. Guy's fantasy bride. And with untied laces and half-buttoned shirt he bolted out of the bedroom, out of the apartment . . . but Guy's harem of apparitions made no attempt at pursuit.

The next morning, Griffin called in sick at work. He was over-tired from not having been able to sleep all night. He had sat up with a kitchen knife in his hand, watching the door and the walls as if some specter or horde of specters might step suddenly through them.

But when it came, the phantom knocked politely at his door. It was a faint, meek knock that he wasn't sure he'd heard at first. Hesitantly but inevitably he went to the door. Cracked it, knife in hand. But then he opened it completely.

For a moment, with the door cracked, he had thought he saw Idelia standing outside, nearly lost in shadow. Her eyes wide and pleading, sad and afraid. A rush of concern or guilt made him open the door all the way. But when he did so, he found that she wasn't there. There was only a swirling pale mist in the general outline of a body, he felt, but which dissipated in moments so that he was left to wonder if it had even been there at all.

SOUL'S NIGHT

JENNIFER RACHEL BAUMER

By the time Cass finally stood to leave the site of the memorial, late afternoon had encompassed the city. She had been sitting on the damp bank of the river for hours, her fingers dug into the earth so she wouldn't fall off. Around her the other mourners had left, singly or in groups, silent people and no one much asked her if she were all right. They had a common purpose. A common loss.

The honor guard had gone sometime after that, somber colors disappearing as afternoon came on. The sun came out and shined dazzlingly off the river where the cask had gone down. For the most part Cass kept her eyes on the spot where she'd last seen it, bobbing for an instant and then sinking beneath the dark waters, much as the plane itself must have sunk. When only the maintenance people were left, airline workers who moved efficiently, stacking chairs, gathering five gallon pots of miniature roses, there was little more attention paid her. A motherly woman with a fluffy Afro stopped beside Cass and tried to convince her to go back to the hotel. Cass stayed silent, her tongue numb. She couldn't talk, couldn't think, and had no reason to head anywhere. Tim was dead and nothing else mattered.

It was supposed to be their second honeymoon. They'd fly out of the city together, vacation somewhere in a tiny locked room. They planned to sleep until noon and make love until three, eat whatever appealed and go to bed at dawn. Two weeks with Tim away from his office and really with her. Really with her. Never with her again.

She came to her feet with a shout, but there was no one around to hear her. They'd all gone and it was late and growing cold. On her feet at last, she shoved her hands into the pocket of Tim's ratty old jacket and made her way down to the water's edge. Just for an instant she imagined jumping in, feeling the cold dark water close over her head as she swam down to the cask and pried the lid loose, lost herself among the mementos of the dead as photographs and white roses floated past her until at last Tim would be there, the black and white she'd had enlarged, showing his grin, his dark eyes, the one chipped tooth that saved him from being overly handsome.

She walked through the city as the afternoon waned. She should go back to her hotel room, go inside. The neighborhoods where she walked were run down, frightening. She shouldn't be here alone. But she couldn't quite remember where the hotel was and she walked until the October sun set and then found her way into a hotel that had a bar and pulled herself up onto one of the seats.

"What'll it be?" The bartender lacked whatever ingredient they were supposed to have to make them the soul of listening. Cass couldn't imagine telling this light eyed man with his oily skin a single thing about her life or what had gone before her subsequent death. She ordered a Manhattan, feeling the irony, but the bartender delivered it without a smile. She decided she didn't like him and started recording little facts to memory, things she'd tell Tim when he got home. When she got home. She shook her head, dizzy. Which one of them was traveling on business?

Had to be her, she thought, and tried to concentrate on what she should be doing, what appointments to keep, what time she'd get home. She smiled a little into her drink, thinking how Tim would welcome her back, how glad to see her he always was.

The drink tasted funny and foreign to her tongue, and somewhat far away. Even the bar was dim, with the music seeming to come through a sweater, fuzzy and incomplete, before reaching her. Cass shook her head again and the world swam. Her first drink, wasn't it? There was only one glass on the bar. But there were four and when the bartender saw her looking his way, he shook his head at her– no more.

I don't want any more, Cass thought. I want to go home. She picked her purse off the bar at the same time someone slid onto the stool next to hers. She heard the end of his sentence,

"–taken?"

and guessed at the rest. Said, "No, and this one isn't either," as she started to slide out.

"Oh, come on, don't be that way," he protested and she looked at the man a little more closely. He looked like Tim a little, kind of sandy haired and stocky. She stopped mid-slide and paused. Maybe not such a big hurry, then. Tim was–

Her head hurt, briefly, buzzed like a hive. Tim was somewhere else. Not here with her. Called away on business, canceled their second honeymoon. That was why she was a little angry with him still. She could taste the leftover anger, like a residue of oil on the tip of her tongue.

"So you alone here?" he asked, this stranger whose eyes were so like Tim's. She could have cried, knowing she'd never see them again. Reached out and put one hand flat on the bar, suddenly afraid she'd fall.

"I buried my husband this afternoon," she said and watched the man's face change. A casual pick up suddenly become a needy woman, suddenly become a story he didn't want to hear. Cass smiled and got a step away from the bar before he spoke again.

"Probably a real bad time to be alone." Almost a question. Definitely a suggestion. Cass squared her shoulders, managed not to laugh or cry.

The streets were cold and wet when she got outside. It had rained since she'd entered the bar, and turned to evening. She drew the collar of Tim's coat up around her throat and struck out for the hotel. She walked through neighborhoods that frightened her, and through streets that were crowded and streets that were empty. She saw Tim in all the faces in the crowd, saw him watching, waiting.

"I'll be home soon," she whispered, and then remembered again, and shook with it.

Midnight came and went and with it another rainstorm fizzled and turned sullen. She didn't know New York. She walked the streets and found herself beside a bridge, no way of knowing if it were famous or not. She could easily lose herself off it. Standing in the cooling night air, she stuck her hands in the pockets of Tim's jacket and this time felt something there. She pulled it out and looked. A ticket stub, something in San Francisco, something long. Cass squinted in the streetlight. A play? She couldn't remember seeing a play with Tim. There were two of them, stuck together, and she turned them over in her hands, noticing a faint lilac perfume.

Memory fluttered and suddenly she was walking very fast, almost running, her shoes slippery on the streets; she'd come dressed for a memorial. Street signs passed her by. She couldn't remember the name of the hotel. Airline putting them up. Offered free transportation, hotel rooms. The other survivors and families, they'd be at the same hotel. Her luggage. She couldn't remember packing, checking in, couldn't remember the room.

"Some place nice," Cass said and slowed down again.

Her heart continued to race.

She woke because Tim had turned over, restless in their bed, woke to put one cool hand on his shoulder, calm his night nerves. He always drifted back then, never remembered in the morning. One more way they were special together.

He'd taken all the covers. She felt cold. The smell of lilacs seemed to invade and she remembered the ticket stubs, holding them in her hand, remembered wanting to ask Tim about them and thought about shaking him awake. Paused. Something wrong. Tried to turn over, move closer.

Memory again. The bed in her hotel room, not at all what she'd have expected of the airline. Had the covers fallen from the bed? She was cold, so cold. Tried to turn over and realized she was standing. Was she sleep walking?

Found herself standing in a park.

She walked faster then, because something was following her, something was catching up. Her blood burned like ice water and she wanted to run, but the memorial shoes– low heeled, sensible– nonetheless had slick soles. She was developing a blister against her right heel, another on her little toe.

Dawn might be coming, she thought. The world wasn't as dark between streetlights. She didn't know what time it was, had lost her watch sometime during the night. She passed people on the streets, dark-eyed and frightening. She thought they watched her and thought they couldn't see her. Their eyes passed her by. She knew she was crying, tears sliding over stained cheeks, her useless fingers straining to press them away, but no one approached her, even when she stopped, even the motherly round woman hosing off the street in front of her bakery.

So it was her, then. She was the one. Cass who had boarded the 747 and taken off in the crisp morning air only to watch as the wing of the plane fell away in slow motion, tumbling down to the dark waters of the East River even as the plane's shadow lunged up at them, a sickening lurch of speed and terror.

Stopped. Watching as the sun rose its way up. Was it? Could she remember back that far, to kissing Tim goodbye, promises of their reuniting, the things they'd do when she returned from that trip?

The memorial shoes slipped and slid, but she was running, fear trailing her, and the streets around her came into focus as the day advanced. She recognized them now, thought she headed, finally, back to her room, back to the hotel where surely the airline had put her up for the memorial in honor of Tim. Running, hard, her feet bleeding into the shoes and one hand clutching those tickets hard enough to bruise her fingers.

The river, suddenly in front of her. She stopped short, one minute in flight, lungs aching, the next minute still. Early sunlight danced off the water, blinding her as she looked for the spot where the cask had gone down. Silent water. Eerie light. Held her breath as memory threatened.

Tickets, in her hand. Tickets not to the play, not the ones she held now, the ones she looked down at and watched twist between sweating fingers. Airline tickets. Tim's. His flight. 1034 to New York. 922 back. And her words, in the air between them. Who is she? Over and over, as if she could say nothing else. Who is she? I know there's someone, Tim, I'm not stupid. Feeling her pulse pound in the back of her skull and Tim's eyes, dark and defenseless. He didn't deny it. There was. There is. Her name is Holly and I love her.

Incredulous. You love me. Feeling her stomach fall as from 20,000 feet. Their personal jokes, their late nights, their speaking without words. He liked salsa in his eggs and always wanted to read magazines first, as if when she read them she somehow deleted their content. He wore socks to bed and brought her roses and always called her when he was going to be late. From the office. From the boardroom.

From the bedroom.

Found herself standing on the muddy bank of the autumn river with the sun rising in painful glory and those ticket stubs, those ghastly proof-giving ticket stubs that smelled like lilac and printed out times and dates when she hadn't been in San Francisco, those stubs clutched tight in her fingers. Tim's face. Not asking forgiveness to come back, not asking for her arms to turn to, but instead, permission to go. Her blessing for him to spend those blessed moments and quiet jokes with someone else.

His airline tickets. Booked, but never taken.

In all the confusion, the airline had contacted her. They were so sorry. There'd been an accident. Tim, gone forever. Their computer should have shown he'd never made the flight, never made either flight, but he'd booked to and from separately, not round trip, and she supposed they didn't care how he'd gotten to New York only to be killed while leaving it.

To be killed while sitting, tense and expectant, his elbows on his knees and his eyes imploring. Never meant to hurt you, Cass.

Never meant to hurt you either, Tim, she thought and let the theater tickets flutter down to the wet ground at her feet. Time to go home, then. Back to their apartment where Tim certainly still lay, the ice pick through his neck, his eyes sightlessly searching hers as if to ask if this were one last shared joke.

Cass walked down to the water's edge, stood staring at the spot where the cask had lowered. Overhead a jet was banking, turning, and heading away into the new morning. Time for her to leave. Time to go home. Time to mourn.

THE ALIEN ARTISTS
ABOUT THE AUTHORS

Jennifer Rachel Baumer writes. Sometimes. Other times she stalls on writing. She writes nonfiction for a living and to support her fiction habit, which she hopes some day will support her. She lives in Reno, Nevada, with her husband Rick and an improbable number of cats. When she's not writing or stalling, she's lifting weights, running, baking, or reading the work of other writers.

Gary A. Braunbeck is the author of nearly two hundred published short stories, seven novels, and nine short story collections, the most recent of which, *Destinations Unknown,* was released by Cemetery Dance Publications this summer. In 2003 Gary's short story "Duty" won the prestigious Bram Stoker Award for Outstanding Achievement in the Short Story. He is currently serving as president of the Horror Writers' Association. Visit him on-line at www.garybraunbeck.com.

Katherine Harbour was born in Albany, New York, and now resides in Sarasota, Florida. She has had thirteen short stories published. She paints dream icons. Hopefully, a book called *Halcyon Summer* is forthcoming.

Ceri Jordan's prose fiction has been widely published in Britain and the US. Her first novel, *Falling,* written under the name Debbie Moon, was short-listed for the Welsh Book of the Year Award 2003. She also writes for film and television. She lives on the west coast of Wales.

Anke Kriske is the author of *A Haven in Winter* (Berkley/Jove), and her stories have appeared in *Cemetery Dance, Woman's World, Alfred Hitchcock's Mystery Magazine,* and *Palace Corbie.* She is also an instructor for a literary correspondence school and an autism activist.

A professional tree-hugger by day, at night *Marc Lecard* writes supernatural short stories and twisted crime comedies. His stories have appeared in *All Hallows, Amazing Journeys,* and on the webzine *Bloodlust UK.* His novel *Vinnie's Head* (St. Martin's Press/Minotaur) will be coming out in April 2007. He lives in South San Francisco.

Seth Lindberg is a writer whose work has appeared in anthologies like *Darker Side* and *Jigsaw Nation,* and an editor for webzines such as *Gothic.net* and, in a short stint, *Chizine.* He currently resides 2700 miles west and 1900 feet below where he was born. You can find out more about him by visiting sethlindberg.com.

Mark McLaughlin is the author of the Delirium Books story collections *Slime After Slime* and *Motivational Shrieker,* and the co-author (with Shane Ryan Staley and Brian Knight) of *At The Foothills Of Frenzy & Other Freakish Forays* from Solitude Publications. Also, he is the co-author (with Rain Graves and David Niall Wilson) of *The Gossamer Eye,* which won a Bram Stoker Award for Poetry.

Kurt Newton grew up in a small house in a small town in Connecticut. He is the author of two short story collections and six collections of poetry. His first novel, *The Wishnik,* was recently published by Delirium Books.

Kate Riedel was born and raised in Minnesota, but now lives in Toronto, Ontario, and has been a card-carrying Canadian for years and years. Publication credits include *On Spec, Realms of Fantasy,* and *Weird Tales.*

Patricia Russo's stories have appeared in *Surreal, City Slab, Tales of the Unanticipated, Fortean Bureau,* and the Stoker Award-nominated anthology *Corpse Blossoms.* "Where I'm from is not my home, and neither's where I'm bound" (Justin Sullivan).

Wayne Allen Sallee's stories have appeared in 169 publications, ranging from crime to horror. This year brings the fifteenth anniversary edition of his novel *The Holy Terror* by Midnight Library, and Annihilation Press will release a new short story collection, *Fiends By Torchlight.*

Sonya Taaffe has a confirmed addiction to myth, folklore, and dead languages. She has had fiction short-listed for the Fountain Award and nominated for the Pushcart Prize, and her poem "Matlacihuatl's Gift" shared first place for the 2003 Rhysling Award. A respectable amount of her short fiction and poetry has recently been collected in *Singing Innocence and Experience* and *Postcards from the Province of Hyphens* (Prime Books). She is currently pursuing a Ph.D. in Classics at Yale University.

Jeffrey Thomas is the author of the novels *Letters From Hades, Everybody Scream!, Monstrocity, Boneland,* and *A Nightmare on Elm Street: The Dream Dealers.* His short story collections include *Punktown, Unholy Dimensions, Punktown: Shades of Grey* (with brother Scott Thomas), and *Thirteen Specimens.* He lives in Massachusetts.

Steve Vernon's novella "Long Horn, Big Shaggy" refuses to die. Steve's collection, *Nothing to Lose* from Nocturne Press, centers on a character so dark he'd give the Batman a case of night fears. Watch for *Four Rode*

Out, a novella collection with Brian Keene, Tim Lebbon, and Tim Curran, due out from Cemetery Dance in late 2007.

ABOUT THE EDITOR

John Benson has been editor and publisher of *Not One of Us* since its debut in 1986. Previously he served as editor of the horror magazine *Doppelgänger*.

In his other life, John is managing director of the opinion research program at the Harvard School of Public Health. He designs and analyzes surveys on public attitudes and knowledge about biological threats, such as avian flu, SARS, mad cow disease, and anthrax, and writes journal articles on these and other domestic policy issues. One of his main research interests is attitudes about end-of-life decisions. John is currently co-editing a book titled *American Public Opinion and Health Policy* (CQ Press).

John's poems have appeared in such magazines as *Tales of the Talisman, Jabberwocky* (with co-author Sonya Taaffe), *The Third Alternative, Tales of the Unanticipated,* and *The Urbanite* (where he and co-author Tina Reigel were featured poets).

John lives in Massachusetts with his wife, two sons, and a strange cat. He has been trying for much of his adult life to disprove the old adage, "You can't hurt a Benson by hitting him in the head."

PUBLICATION HISTORY

"Another Coming" by Sonya Taaffe first appeared in *Not One of Us* 32, September 2004.

"The Elevator" by Patricia Russo first appeared in *Not One of Us* 27, March 2002.

"Matters of Family" by Gary A. Braunbeck first appeared in *Not One of Us* 5, August 1989.

"There the Great City Stands" by Ceri Jordan first appeared in *Not One of Us* 17, February 1997.

"Night Window" by Marc Lecard first appeared in *Not One of Us* 31, April 2004.

"Chad" by Kate Riedel first appeared in *Not One of Us* 14, September 1995.

"Take the 'A' Train" by Wayne Allen Sallee first appeared in *Not One of Us* [1], October 1986.

"C2" by Anke Kriske first appeared in *Not One of Us* 32, September 2004.

"The Rosegarden" by Seth Matthew Lindberg first appeared in *Not One of Us* 23, March 2000.

"Fading" by Katherine Harbour first appeared in *Not One of Us* 13, February 1995.

"The Birthday Ritual" by Kurt Newton first appeared in *Not One of Us* 13, February 1995.

"The Last Poetry Night at the Saturnalia Coffee House" by Mark McLaughlin first appeared in *Not One of Us* 11, November 1993.

"Hooney Jew, Hooney Jew" by Steve Vernon first appeared in *Not One of Us* 8, October 1991.

"Pale Fruit" by Jeffrey Thomas first appeared in *Not One of Us* 22, September 1999.

"Soul's Night" by Jennifer Rachel Baumer first appeared in *Not One of Us* 27, March 2002.

www.ingramcontent.com/pod-product-compliance
Lightning Source LLC
Chambersburg PA
CBHW022215050726

47590CB00002B/803